TUNN VISIONS

S Blockley
&
D J Thacker

Copyright © 2024 S Blockley & D J Thacker

All rights reserved.

The characters and events portrayed in this book are fictitious. Any similarity to real persons, living or dead, is coincidental and not intended by the authors.

No part of this book may be reproduced, or stored in a retrieval system, or transmitted in any form or by any means, electronic, mechanical, photocopying, recording, or otherwise, without express written permission of the publisher or authors.

ISBN – 13: 9798883296757

All photographs taken by the authors

Other Publications by S Blockley & D J Thacker:

The Welsh Hercules

By David J Thacker:

Once: A Belmouth Tale

The Red House / The Last Rat Child

All titles available on Amazon

Introduction

People Make Glasgow says the slogan, but the reverse is also true: Glasgow makes people.

It's a great sprawling city – not as romantic, perhaps, as Edinburgh, and it doesn't even have a castle, like Stirling – but for those of us who call it home, we wouldn't have anywhere else. It's a city of diversity, welcoming to all, and it gives shelter and life to a variety of characters within it.

Although the Clyde runs through it, it's the subway that binds it. When we set out to tell stories that would give a feel of this great city, of the people within it, we realised that we would need some kind of connecting thread for them. The subway seemed the obvious choice (and, as far as we can see, it hasn't been used in this way before). It allowed us as writers to visit different areas and different classes of people, even different time periods. It shaped the stories of some characters while for others it was just a background feature. It is part of the everyday life of Glasgow and touches everyone in the city.

The Glasgow Subway system, for those that don't know, is a closed loop. You can hop on a train going in either direction and always end up at your destination. We'd like to think it's the same with our stories – you can read them in order, travelling along the route of the Inner Circle from the City Centre, out across the river, and back again, or you can choose a stop and explore that area. Along the way, you can find heartbreak, salvation, a dash of fantasy, a pinch of history, high art and low humour – just as you can on the streets of the city itself.

Whatever way you choose to read the book, though, we hope you enjoy it. This is our second outing as co-authors (the first, *The Welsh Hercules*, is also available from Amazon) and we'd love to know what you think of it. You can contact us on Instagram (@tunnel_visions_glasgow).

Now jump on board, the train is about to leave...

S Blockley & D J Thacker

Contents

Buchanan Street	09
Cowcaddens	25
St George's Cross	49
Kelvinbridge	69
Hillhead	89
Kelvinhall (Partick Cross)	105
Partick	123
Govan	137
Ibrox	151
Cessnock	165
Kinning Park	177
Shields Road	191
West Street	207
Bridge Street	221
St Enoch	239

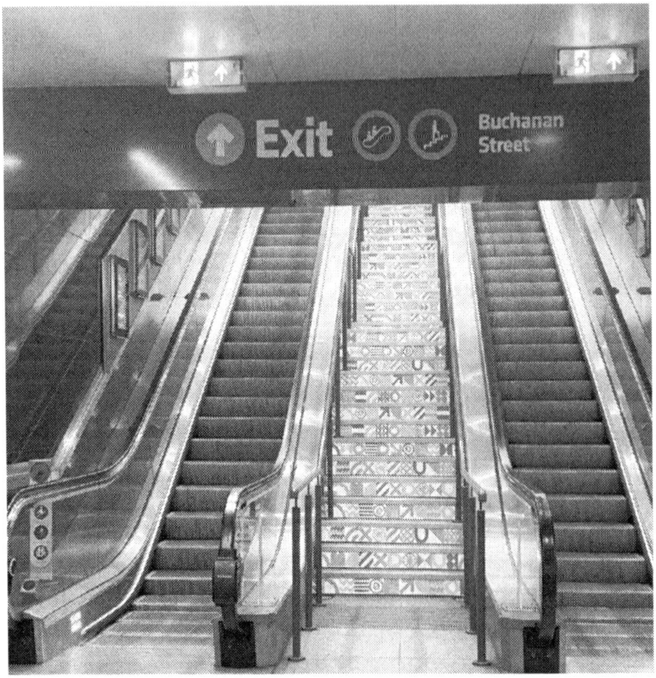
Exit
Buchanan
Street

Kinning Park to **Buchanan Street**

The train pulled away from the Kinning Park platform and immediately he felt his heart beat faster. For the second time he glanced around the carriage.

He'd checked when he'd first stepped on board, of course, so realistically he knew she wasn't there. But habit made him look again.

No, the coast was clear.

It had only happened once before. She had got on two stops before him as usual and he'd not even looked at the carriage windows as the train pulled in. He'd been scanning for a seat, with the doors closing behind him, when he'd seen her. Further down the carriage, beyond the next set of doors. Just sitting, looking ahead. Oblivious of him. He had willed her to not look around, desperately hoping she wouldn't see him. He didn't want that spark of recognition, the awkwardness that would follow. He didn't want the longing to pierce both of them.

That journey to the next stop had taken forever, seconds stretching into hours. He could have turned around, he realised later, presented his back to her, but he couldn't bear to look away. As soon as the doors opened, he was off the train, standing on the platform, watching the doors close again and thanking any god that would listen that he had not been seen. That *they* had not been seen.

This trip was fine, though. He would have to watch out when they arrived at Buchanan Street station, in case she was in any of the other carriages emptying out onto the platform around him, but they both knew the deal. Outside of the meeting place, they were strangers to each other – and somehow it was easier to pretend that with people milling around them, all jostling to get to the ticket barriers, than when he was in an enclosed space with her.

For now, however, he could relax and prepare to meet her properly, openly, in just five stops time.

She arrived early to the Costa Coffee shop on George Square, as she always did these days. She wanted to be there first, to get her coffee and find a suitable table. She wanted somewhere away from the windows, quiet enough to talk and not be overheard and with a good view of the doors. That way, she could see him arrive, and watch for anyone else who might walk in.

The girl behind the counter smiled at her in a way that suggested she recognised her face. Perhaps it was time to find another place to meet. It had been eight months since they had first come here, that initial awkward rendezvous, and they had been meeting once a week every week since. It was only natural the staff would get to know their faces. She wasn't sure if that could be a problem or not. Perhaps it was a decision they both needed to make.

Both. As the thought crossed her mind, she smiled slightly at the use of the term. Evidently, they were now established enough to make joint decisions. It was a strange and slightly frightening thought, and yet also curiously comforting.

All the same, she did not order for him as well. She knew exactly what he would be drinking (a latte with a sprinkle of chocolate on it), but she was not yet ready to acknowledge that she could do this for him. Perhaps after this weekend they would be at that stage, but not now. Not while it was still innocent.

She smiled back at the girl and placed her order.

He saw her sat at their usual table and waited in the queue to order his drink. He glanced over to her and she smiled back. Just that made it all worth it.

He ordered his latte with a sprinkle of chocolate on top. It was a drink he didn't have at any other time. At their first meeting here, the server had made a mistake, thinking she was preparing a cappuccino, but he told her to leave it. Now it was the drink he had with her – something different and just slightly special.

He took the drink over to the table and they kissed. Chaste, peck on the cheek kisses, but it still made him happy. It meant he was close enough to feel the warmth of her skin, to catch her perfume. A promise not a tease.

"How are you?" he asked.

"Oh, I'm fine," she answered. She was looking straight at him. No deception now. This was their space and within it they could be who they really wanted to be. At least to a degree. "You?"

He smiled. "Can't complain. Especially now."

His hand brushed the back of hers and it was electric.

"How's Marie?" she asked. "And Tom."

They had said right from the start that they would talk about their partners. He was married with a 13-year old son. She had been with the same man for twelve years, not formally married but still with two children. Both of them knew the other would never – could never – leave their partner so they acknowledged it.

That was one life. This was another.

"She's good," he said. "Tom's having a bit of trouble at school…"

For a while, they talked about family things. Anyone casually observing them would have thought they were friends meeting up after a period apart. Except if they looked closely, they might have seen the affectionate touches that played between them both, the small but meaningful glances, the smiles that weren't connected to what was said but to who was speaking.

The conversation paused naturally. Neither felt the need to break the silence but finally he said, "It's coming up to Christmas again."

She looked at him, a playful look. It made him giddy.

"Our anniversary, I suppose."

He nodded.

They had met at the company Christmas Party. There was an open bar and, as this was most people's first major social event since the pandemic, the drink was flowing freely.

He didn't know many people there. He was still working from home – one of those roles that couldn't possibly be done remotely until it had to be – and the only people he knew were in his Teams Group. She had returned to office work but wasn't interested in getting drunk with people she would later need to supervise. They met at the bar and struck up a conversation.

The attraction had been immediate, but neither wanted to act on it. They chatted easily, finding common ground without having to search for it. They discussed work briefly, then moved on to their home lives. So different yet so alike. Both teasing small confessions out of the other – he doesn't understand me anymore, I've grown apart from her – fuelled by alcohol, anonymity and relief at being able to say it aloud.

At the end of the night, they had been drunk enough to swap numbers but not to go any further. They went their separate ways and that should have been the end of it.

Except two days later, heart in his mouth, he texted her.

She replied within five minutes. They continued chatting, moving over to WhatsApp after a week. They came to know each other's patterns – he had football on a Thursday, one of her children had a dance class on a Saturday morning. It was exciting and secret. It was dangerous and all-consuming.

And it was theirs, something away from home and work and stagnant lives, something to make them feel alive again.

After a month of furtive texts and heartbreakingly long silences, he knew that he had to see her again. For a coffee, he promised. Nothing more.

So now, eight months later, they were here and on the edge of breaking that promise.

"We could wait until Christmas," she said. "If you want."

"No. No," he replied, worried that his answer was too quick, too eager. "Unless, of course, you are having second thoughts…"

She shook her head. "No. Not at all." She took a beat, wondered whether to say it. Then: "I don't want to wait."

He felt a grin spread across his face at the words. She looked at him and smiled back.

"What excuse have you given?" she asked.

"A colleague's birthday," he said. "And it is. Jim from my team. But he's not doing anything for it."

"I said it was a girl's night out and I'd be staying over with Jenny rather than wake everyone," she said. "Jenny knows about us, so she'll cover if need be."

This was new. He hadn't told anyone about her, keeping it something just between them, something sealed away from every other concern. For her to have told someone else seemed strange. He wasn't worried about the secret getting out – if she trusted her friend, he would too – but, somehow, sharing what they had diminished it.

"I've booked the room," he said.

They looked at one another. For a moment, what they were doing hit both of them. The excitement left their eyes and concern flooded in. Doing this made everything real. It was no longer just a weekly chat, hidden longings. It was action. It could break their worlds.

She shook her head to clear it and he noticed the way a whisp of hair fell across her eyes, the offhand way that she pushed it back into place, and this small gesture banished all that had gone before it. She was beautiful and he ached to hold her.

She looked into his eyes and saw the desire there. It had been a long time since she had seen that at home. It made her feel alive and seen.

Their fingers touched on the table and neither of them pulled back.

He knew that he couldn't text her – shouldn't text her – but he wanted to. It was 11am on Saturday morning; she'd be with her daughter at dance class and that meant she couldn't answer him. Still, it pulled at him, the fact that he couldn't speak to her, couldn't confirm that everything was still good for that evening.

There was no reason to think it wouldn't be. The hotel was booked (he'd already checked the booking confirmation on his phone three times that morning). He would see her in just a few hours. When they had parted in the week, it had all been planned.

Now it just had to happen.

His gym bag was in the hall by the door. Everything ready to go. Well, almost. He planned to call into the chemists on the way to the Subway station and buy some condoms. Better than having them in the bag and Marie finding them.

He had decided he would leave the house around 2pm. Marie thought he was travelling over to Stirling for the night, so it fitted with that story, but in reality he knew he couldn't access the hotel room any earlier than that. She was arriving at around 5pm, meeting him at the hotel. They had decided on the Premier Inn on George Street, not so far away from where all their coffee meetings had been. Still on familiar ground.

Three hours to kill. It sounded like such a short time.

"Where are you going again, Mum?" Ellie, her youngest was the inquisitive type.

They were in the foyer of the Dance School. All the parents waited there whilst their children, invariably girls, pirouetted and plié'd beyond a forbidding set of doors. After class, the young dancers returned to this spot to get changed.

"It's just a girl's night out," she said. "With Aunty Jenny."

"But where?" the girl persisted. "Where are you going?"

She hadn't really put much thought into specifics like that. For a moment, she felt a panic flood her body, but she fought it back. "We're just going into Glasgow. Going to a few bars. We'll see where the night takes us."

The little girl nodded sagely, evidently satisfied with the extra detail.

All the same, lying to her daughter brought a slight lump to her throat. Speaking to her partner about it had caused no such qualms – he had hardly been listening anyway and seemed to care even less – but she had always tried to bring her children up to do the right thing. To be honest.

It gave her a moment's pause.

The station was surprisingly quiet for a Saturday afternoon. Signs warned of busier platforms later in the day when the football came out, but for now hardly anyone else was waiting with him.

He put his Metro card in his coat pocket and his hand brushed against the packet of condoms. He grabbed them and put them in the gym bag before anyone could see. He had thought long and hard about getting them. They hadn't spoken about it but he felt that he should. Better to have them and for the night to go smoothly than to not have them and it be a problem.

Even so, he knew that it was just a small part of their evening ahead. He looked forward to being naked with her, of course, but he also longed to just hold her, to sleep next to her, to spoon with her. Even waking the next morning and going down to breakfast together was a wonderful thought.

Breakfast that morning had been prickly. He had been eager to get away and that translated into being irritable with Marie. He felt as if she was blocking his day just by being there. It was irrational and he knew it, but they still ended up sniping at each other all the same.

When he had come to leave, he could see relief in her eyes just as he assumed she could see it in his. He'd kissed her goodbye but more as a duty than anything else. It wasn't her he wanted to be kissing.

But now he was on his way. Free, even if it had been bought with a lie. The pent-up anger, the frustration he'd felt at home, had dissipated almost as soon as he had reached the station. He could breathe again.

The train pulled in and he got on board, leaving any lingering doubts on the platform behind him.

Once again, she was there, at their usual table, as he arrived. There were two coffees in front of her, one with a sprinkle of chocolate.

She stood as he approached. He went in to kiss her on the mouth but something happened and his lips just grazed her cheek instead. Before he could try again, she had sat back down.

"How are you?" she said.

"Not as good as I was on Saturday night," he replied and smiled. She smiled back and a blush spread across her cheeks.

"Not as nervous," she said.

It was true. When they had met in the hotel lobby, he had looked anxious. It had always been the plan that he arrived early, picked up the room key and found out where the room was. Then he was to meet her in the foyer and together they would ride up to the room - less a romantic gesture and more a necessity as the hotel lifts required a key card.

When they got to the room, they had kissed. Their first full kiss, holding one another, melting into the other person. But she had been surprised to feel him shaking slightly. Tense shivers that slowly receded as the kiss lasted, grew, progressed into buttons being undone, clothes coming off.

Now he smiled bashfully at her gentle teasing. "I recovered, though," he said.

She took a sip of her coffee. "You did."

She asked if there had been any trouble when he had returned home the next day, knowing the answer from their texts but wanting to bring his focus back to his real life. She told him about going home herself, talking with her friend about her cover story, lying to her partner, to her children.

Throughout their conversation, he watched her. He always had – they had both always enjoyed the illicit thrill of being together in public, of being so close yet unable to really touch the other, of having to study their looks, their mannerisms, instead – but now he was more open about it. Or perhaps she just noticed it more.

Eventually it came to the question.

"When do you think we can do it again?" he said. "Do you think you can get away at Christmas?"

She looked at him. This was the part she had been dreading.

"I don't think we should," she said.

He looked at her. She had never really understood the word dumbfounded until that moment.

"But... why? Did I do something wrong?"

Her mind betrayed her, showing memories of sheets caught on naked bodies, of the tang of a stranger's sweat, of passion met with passion.

"No, nothing wrong," she said.

But how could she explain her decision?

You live for this moment, she wanted to say. You exist in the Now of our time together and any future you see is based on this little bubble we share.

This 'other life' is becoming more real to you than your actual life.

Whereas I see further down the line. I see Discovery. Heartache. Loss. The truth is we can't sustain this secret and so I have to break it up now, before it gets out of hand, before it gets messy. Before I fall in love with you. Because what we want cannot happen. We have families, responsibilities. Reality. And all we have here is a wonderful, beautiful fantasy.

She wanted to say this but she didn't think she'd have the strength to do it, to expose his dream to the cruel light she saw it in. She knew she was going to hurt him but there was no need to take everything away from him.

He was starting to speak again, but she put her hand over his on the table. He stopped and she was struck by just what a prosaic setting this was for decisions that would change lives.

"I can't let this happen," she said. "I hope you'll understand. If not now, then later. But I just can't let it happen."

She lifted her hand from his and stood up.

"Trust me when I say this hurts. Hurts more than I ever thought it could. What we had, what we did, what we were, is something I'll never forget. You are someone I'll never forget. But there's no future in it."

He wanted to argue but part of him knew what she was saying. His body had told him when they had met at the hotel. They should never have taken that step, should never have left this coffee shop. Here it was all promise and potential. Saturday had somehow taken that away from them.

Still, he wanted to fight for her, to win her back.

"I'll text you," he said.

She shook her head and pulled on her coat.

"Don't. I won't answer." It was one of the hardest things she'd ever said.

As she passed him to leave, he grabbed her wrist. She looked down at him and he saw the tears in her eyes. He knew that he could hold her there, perhaps even convince her to sit back down, but it would only bring more tears and he didn't want to hurt her. Not any more than they had already hurt each other. He opened his fingers and let her go.

As she walked out the door, refusing to look back, she knew it was for the best, for both of them. For their families. She set off back towards Buchanan Street, pulling her coat around her against a suddenly cold and empty day.

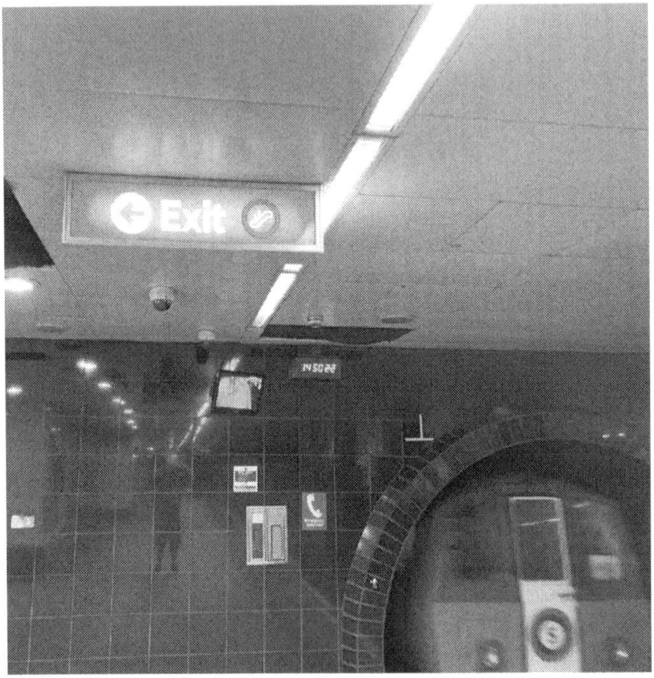
Exit
14 50 02

Kelvinbridge to **Cowcaddens**

She could feel the subway train slowing down. Must be a problem on the tracks, she thought. Or maybe at Cowcaddens station.

Nicola glanced at her watch. There was still plenty of time to make it to the rehearsal. The carriage seemed a little quieter now that the train had slowed. She could make out the noise of the wheels going over the tracks rather than just the deafening rush of air through the tunnels.

A dull thud. Then another. Another. A perfect beat.

It was hardly noticeable, but her mind picked up on it. 4/4 time - another slight clunk from the wheels making the quarter notes, repeating regularly. Unconsciously her fingers tapped out the rhythm on her jeans as she sat in the carriage. Shuffle Blues timing, she realised - and with that came a song. Robert Johnson singing 'Kind Hearted Woman Blues'. Nicola started to hum along to the beat in her head even as the train picked up speed again and the tempo outside was lost.

She closed her eyes and the lyrics floated in front of her, teasing her into singing along. It was a good song, a favourite, even if the lyrics weren't suited to a female singer. *Like so much in this industry*, she thought. But that wouldn't stop her singing it if she could convince Mike that it should be in the set.

She could sell it as gender-bending, or appealing to their LGBTQ+ fans, or just being radical - she was sure he'd go for one of those. It just took timing. Knowing when to introduce the idea. But she was sure she could do it.

The train shuddered to a halt and Nicola stood to get off. As she stepped out onto the platform, the song was still arranging itself in her head to a version she could work best with.

As she stepped into the cold outside Cowcaddens station, Nicola heard her phone ping softly. Rain was in the air, so she waited until she had gotten around the corner and under the shelter of the subway tunnel before checking what it was.

Another subscriber to her YouTube channel. Nicola smiled to herself - not much longer and she'd be at 2000 followers. Plus her latest music video had been seen by 3200 people and it had only been up for 10 days. Things were on the up!

She had always been active on social media but these days, if you wanted a career in music, it was essential. Agents wouldn't look at you if you didn't bring a hefty online presence and proven followers. A lot of promotion these days was left to the artist rather than some Media guru.

Which in one sense levelled the playing field - but it also meant that people on the start of the ladder, like her, had to spend a lot of time online instead of where they wanted to be - on stage or in a studio. Luckily, Nicola quite enjoyed this side of the business too.

She posted to YouTube and, in shortened versions, TikTok. She was pretty active on Twitter (or whatever it called itself these days) and followed lots of local venues and national artists, making sure to comment on any issues that could emphasise her songwriting or music credentials. She excelled on Instagram, with over 9000 followers from across the world. Nicola was aware that she had picked up quite a lot of these from her looks rather than her art - her dark hair and olive skin leant her a Mediterranean or even Latino air that was internationally pleasing. Even so, she was careful with what she posted. She didn't agree with the viewpoint that all female artists had to be beautiful - male artists could achieve fame through their songwriting skills and the quality of their voices, whereas women, no matter how good they were, had to look good as well or no one would entertain using them. Yes, she knew she *was* naturally good looking, but that shouldn't have to be a factor in her success. Her talent should be the strongest thing about her.

If she was honest, as well, the other aspect of putting her looks out there online was that it scared her. Or the reaction to it did. A year ago, she had posted a picture whilst on holiday. She had been on the beach and wearing a very modest bikini. A girlfriend had taken it and she'd liked the fact that, caught candidly, she looked relaxed and happy. Two hours later, she checked her feed and was shocked at the comments it had attracted. Lewd jokes and frank sexual statements flooded her timeline. Total strangers made comments that she wouldn't even have accepted from a boyfriend. None of them saw the same things she did in the picture - she was just a piece of meat on display. She had taken the post down immediately and from that moment on stayed with only chaste and clothed pictures.

Now, however, Nicola was able to put her phone away and smile at her current good fortune. For once, it really seemed like her work was winning out and she was starting to get noticed for the right reasons. And tonight could only improve on that.

"Paul, can you make it a bit more Buddy Guy and a bit less Deon Estus, please?" Mike was giving notes at the end of the rehearsal and as usual he had some for their resident bass player.

"Nothing wrong with Deon," Paul muttered.

"It's just I'm trying to get that traditional Chicago blues feel here," Mike continued. "But it keeps moving more towards funk with your bass. Funk is not bad, it's just not what we want for a Howlin' Wolf song."

"I'll try," Paul replied, sullenly.

Mike turned away from the band. His singer was sat in a corner of the rehearsal room, swigging from a water bottle.

"Nic," he called. "Really well done. Giving it those Joss Stone vibes." Mike gave a thumbs up in her direction.

Nicola smiled back and raised the bottle in a mock toast. On the one hand, she was quite pleased with the comparison to one of her favourite singers; on the other hand, she wasn't wild about someone who used the word 'vibes'.

It summed up her relationship with Mike. Since joining the band four months ago, Nicola had found its leader to be a polarising influence. On the one hand, he was a good keyboardist, and he knew his stuff. He was a huge Blues fan and had an almost encyclopaedic knowledge of the genre. Most people (if they thought about it at all) assumed the name of the band, The Moneymakers, was a reference to the famous Elmore James song, but Mike had confided to her one night after practise that it was actually taken from an earlier track by Shakey Jake Harris. Nicola prided herself on a pretty good knowledge of blues singers, but even she had never heard of that one.

So, Mike knew music and moreover he cared about music and he kept a pretty tight ship with the band, insisting on regular rehearsals and commitment. Plus, he was also good at getting them gigs. Nicola worked her own live sets away from the band, mostly wedding gigs or pub nights, covering some of her other idols like Mariah Carey or her Mum's favourite, Shirley Bassey. They were her bread and butter, musically speaking, but her regular nights with The Moneymakers, those were the icing on the cake. As a band, they played actual venues, either as part of an ensemble evening or as support for a headliner. These were the gigs that would get her noticed. And the pay was better too.

However, there were other sides to Mike that she didn't find as palatable. In displaying his fervent love of the blues, he often strayed into being pretentious and inflexible. Differing points of view were rarely considered and, although he did know how to make a tune swing, he wasn't as keen on giving bandmembers much leeway to explore their own improvisations within it. This was at the centre of his problems with Paul. Nicola knew that the bassist was already looking for another group to join and she knew it would only be a matter of time before The Moneymakers would be placing another ad similar to the one that had found her.

"You coming to MacConnell's for a pint?" Mike asked.

If she was honest with herself, this was the reason Nicola had moved over to a corner on her own once the rehearsal had finished. She wasn't averse to a drink with the band after a session – what musician ever was? – but she was wary of it when Mike asked.

"I might just have some interesting news if you do," he continued, giving her a sly wink that did nothing to quell her misgivings.

Paul and Keith, the lead guitarist, both looked up at this statement and were evidently as puzzled by it as she was. Davey, their resident drummer was busy putting his kit away, so he may not have heard the comment. Then again, he was a man of few words, so it was difficult to tell.

Perhaps it would be worth it. "Yeah, I'll be there," Nicola said, and hoped she wouldn't regret it.

MacConnell's was a lively pub on the opposite corner of the street to the Theatre Royal. As the band arrived, the theatre audience was just leaving and the street was filled with spirited chatter as groups discussed the evening's performance or bade each other goodnight. Few of them would be heading into the pub, though – it wasn't really for the Theatre crowd.

Nicola liked it. Yes, they had giant screens showing the football, and yes, it was a bit rough around the edges, but it was homely and they did live music and karaoke on occasions. The bar staff were friendly, and the beer was good. They were even able to find a reasonably quiet corner to talk.

The five of them sat around a small table.

"Go on then," Keith said, eventually. "What is it you want to tell us?" Out of all of them, Keith was probably the one most eager to leave. A lifelong Rangers supporter, he was no fan of the green and white livery around the bar.

Mike took a sip of his pint and smiled at them. *He's enjoying playing this out*, Nicola thought. *Twat*.

"You know that I have a drink with Charlie Franks occasionally?" he said finally.

Everyone did know this. Charlie Franks was one of the biggest music promoters in Glasgow and everybody in the business locally wanted to be on his good side. Reading between the lines, Nicola had worked out that previous tales of 'drinks with Charlie' had actually meant 'drinking in the same establishment as Charlie', but she was willing to let the distinction slide if it kept Mike happy and meant he kept his ear to the ground.

"Well," Mike continued, "There's going to be an audition to be the support act for a headliner at the SECC in a month's time – and I've got us a slot in it!"

Everyone looked at him in shock for a moment. Then Paul broke the silence.

"Who is it?"

"Apparently, Charlie is contractually obliged not to say – but he will say that it's a local guy who's done well, very well – several Number Ones well! – and who has already sold the place out. He wants to give back to the community or something and so wants an up-and-coming local band to open for him."

Everybody knew who Mike was talking about. There could only be one artist with that description and whose music would fit with theirs.

"Fuck!" Keith said quietly.

"Indeed," Mike said, taking another swig of his beer. "I mean, it's by no means ours and there are eight bands auditioning over two days, but it's worth a crack – and if nothing else, it brings us further into Charlie's eyeline."

"How many nights is it?" Keith asked.

"He's playing three nights and they'd rather use just one band throughout," Mike said. "It's a thirty minute set and our, well, the winner's name will be on the posters."

The band sat for a moment, thinking about it. At least, everyone assumed Davey was thinking about it – he hadn't spoken a word yet and the curtain of long hair over his face made it difficult to tell if he was even awake.

"You're very quiet, Nic" Mike said. As he was sitting next to her, he used it as an excuse to place one hand on her knee.

Gently, Nicola removed it.

"How many songs do we need for the audition?" she asked.

"Two," Mike replied. He didn't seem upset by the rebuttal. He'd had enough of them from Nicola by now.

That was the other thing Nicola didn't like about Mike. She was pretty sure he had hired her originally because he wanted to get off with her. It was a trope of the business that actors were often asked to try out the Casting Couch with a Producer / Director / Backer, but it was less well-known in the music industry. Which is not to say it didn't happen, because it very definitely did, just that it was not as frequently discussed. All the same, it wasn't something Nicola was willing to do.

She had to admit that Mike was easy on the eye, but it just wasn't her way. Fair play to the girls (and boys) who did take that route, but she knew her talent would last longer than a quick shag. Despite this, Mike never seemed to give up. He wasn't yet moving into Sex Pest territory, but he was circling the region.

"How about 'Sweet Home Chicago' and 'Just Make Love To Me'? They're crowd pleasers," Nicola suggested.

"Good choices," Mike said, and his hand returned to her knee. "We can discuss it later, though. The audition's not for two weeks. We've got plenty of time."

This time Nicola didn't remove his hand, but she was prepared to if it moved above her knee. She needed this break and she needed Mike to listen to her, to give her a set that would showcase her voice. For that, she needed to stay on his good side, no matter how much she disliked compromising a few morals. It was too much to hope that they would use one of her own songs, but at least she could have a say in the standards they covered.

"Very true," she said. "Anyone for another round?"

A week later and the set had been chosen and rehearsals were well underway.

Initially, Nicola had not been wild about Mike's choice of songs. He had vetoed her choices on the grounds that 'Sweet Home Chicago' had been "done to death, and not always well" and 'Just Make Love To Me' was "too niche". In Nicola's mind, this only allowed them to show their versatility – by giving new life to a standard and showcasing a little-known classic – but her arguments fell on deaf ears. Probably, she reflected, she had spoken too soon, showed too much eagerness. Mike didn't want anyone else putting their stamp on his band.

Instead, they went with Albert King's 'Born Under A Bad Sign' (*Yeah, like that one hadn't been done to death*, Nicola thought, but she had to admit it did allow the band to shine) and, in a surprise move, 'Didn't It Rain, Children' by Sister Rosetta Tharpe. Now that was more like it – a genuine classic from the Mother of Rock 'n Roll and a song that would showcase her vocals beautifully. Plus, it was a genuine crowd pleaser.

"You look tired, Nic" Paul said to her at the end of a rehearsal.

To be fair she was. Working as a Teaching Assistant during the day, then rehearsing, or recording her own demos at home, every night was starting to take its toll. On top of that, she had a booking for a Fortieth Birthday Party on Saturday and she still hadn't learned a couple of favourite songs that the Birthday boy's spouse had asked for.

"Ach, I'll be fine," she said. "Only another week to go."

Paul gave her what she considered a Dad Look but didn't pursue the subject any further.

"Our glorious leader is being a bit shifty, don't you think?" he said instead.

Nicola glanced across at Mike who seemed to be trying to talk to Davey. As usual, it was difficult to tell if this was a conversation with or just at the drummer.

"How do you mean?" she asked.

"Dunno, just something off," the bass player replied. "I asked if we could swap one of the rehearsal nights but he point blank refused. Said he was already busy that night. I mean, when have you ever known Mike to have a life outside the band?"

It was odd. "Well, perhaps he's learning to grow as a person," Nicola said with a wink. "I believe they do therapy sessions in an evening now."

"Jeezo, he'd be telling the therapist where he was going wrong before the first hour was up!" Paul smiled. "Aye, maybe."

Nicola took another swig of her water and shrugged off his concerns. She had enough to think about as it was without worrying about Mike's comings and goings.

Two days later, Nicola had cause to think of that conversation again.

The Birthday gig had gone quite well. It was always awkward being the act who was on when the food was being brought out, but, Nicola reflected, those were the breaks. She had chosen her backing tapes carefully and started the set quietly – modern standards that everybody knew but which weren't too distracting. Just background music. There was no point in throwing in the big guns when the dominant noise in the function suite was the clack of cutlery on plates. But as the meal progressed, she slowly amped up the tempo of the songs and moved into singalong territory. A few early finishers (and some of the waiting staff) joined in and by the time most people had finished the dessert course, she had become the star attraction.

That was when she moved into the covers of songs that had been requested, belting out a Streisand hit and a ballad from Adele before ending on her own choice, P!nk's 'Get The Party Started'. By that point everyone was on their feet and Nicola was able to hand the evening over to the DJ who would take the crowd into the small hours of the morning.

The client was extremely happy, even giving her a £50 tip (Nicola was sure alcohol played its part in this generosity, but she wasn't about to turn it down) and to top it off there was a free meal waiting for her.

All in all, a good night, but now all she wanted was her bed, an episode of *Love Island* and some hot chocolate. The rest of the world could go hang for one night.

Standing on the Partick Subway platform, all Nicola could think about was putting her feet up. The platform was fairly busy so she didn't expect to get a seat on the train, and that only made her desire to get home all the stronger. Across the way from her, the Outer line train pulled away, leaving an empty platform and a few stragglers making their way up the escalators.

As she watched, a couple came running down the other escalator, only to find that they had missed the train. Nicola wasn't really paying them any attention, but suddenly the man stepped into view and she realised that it was Mike.

Her interest now piqued, Nicola looked again. Yes, definitely Mike. And he was definitely with the young blonde woman beside him. He turned and pulled her in close to him, one arm around her waist. The blonde made a token gesture of fighting him off, then leaned in for a quick kiss. Well, that was a surprise – but it explained Mike's business away from the band.

There was something familiar about the girl as well, something Nicola couldn't put her finger on. Perhaps it would come to her later.

She shook her head to clear it but as Nicola looked up again her own train pulled in to the station and the couple were wiped from her view. Well, it was none of her business, anyway, she thought as the doors opened in front of her and the crowd surged forwards.

By the time she had gotten on the train and found a suitable place to stand in the crush, Nicola had forgotten all about the girl.

This was why she did it.

This was why she put up with people eating a meal while she was singing, why she played small pubs where no one was listening or weddings where all they wanted was whatever was Number One that week. This was worth the late nights, the poor pay, the groping and the assumptions that the only way for her to succeed was on her back.

Nicola stood on stage for the audition and felt the music surround her, caress her, and then release itself through the combined efforts of all the members of the band.

This was living.

'Born Under A Bad Sign' stutter-rocked itself to an end and Nicola knew they all felt the same. It was almost a religious experience – shared, collaborative and yet also more than the sum of its parts.

Without really pausing, Paul's foot tapped a beat on the floor and counted Keith's guitar in to start the Sister Rosetta Tharp song. This was her moment. It didn't matter that the band was only playing to ten people in a cavernous room, or that there were three other bands waiting in the wings for their turn. It didn't even matter that this was a pivotal moment in all their careers. All that mattered was the song. Getting it right. Selling that emotion, feeling the words.

Nicola opened her mouth and sang.

The wait was excruciating. As they had performed on the first of two audition days, Nicola had always known there would be at least a day's grace before any news, but when, at the end of the third day, they had still not heard anything there was very little confidence left to keep her doubts at bay.

There was no rehearsal that week, partly because the amped-up schedule of the past two weeks had left everyone tired and partly because the band didn't want to get back together until they knew what was happening. No one had said it, but it felt like bad luck to meet before then.

So, effectively, she was on her own. Waiting.

It was just after 8pm when she got the first message.

Nicola had been idly channel-hopping, looking for something on tv to take her mind off the audition. Unfortunately, there only seemed to be a glut of talent shows at that time of night, and all she could find were hopeful wannabes, their smiles shining out of the screen in quiet desperation. It was too close to home to be enjoyable.

Her phone softly pinged by the side of her and she quickly picked it up. It was a WhatsApp message from Paul. She read it, and then read it again.

Bloody Hell! Big Time here we come!

Did that mean..? Nicola didn't dare hope on such a flimsy message. But, what else could it mean? Had they won the audition? If so, why hadn't Mike contacted her?

She could feel her heart beating faster. She knew she was getting her hopes up, but she also couldn't fight the excitement that was building within her. Nicola looked around the room as if that could give her an answer. She stood up, needing something to do, and started to pace the room.

Another ping. This time a message from Keith.

Fuuuuuuuuuck!!!

Nicola smiled and immediately the smile turned to a laugh. She found herself staring at the phone screen and just giggling at the message. They'd done it! They had to have done it!

Nicola swiped the message away and started to send a new message to Mike. As she did so, the message *typing...* appeared under Mike's name. About bloody time, Nicola thought, and stopped her own text until she'd seen what he had to say.

Mike seemed to be typing for a long time. By the time his message did come through, Nicola was already thinking of how much shit she was going to give him at the next rehearsal for leaving her until last.

You've probably heard by now that The Moneymakers were successful in winning the place as the opening act for next month's concert at the SECC. A lot of that success was down to you and the way you lead the band, which makes it doubly difficult for me to have to tell you that I have decided the band needs a change in direction for this new phase in its story. I feel the band needs someone who can get a crowd up and dancing on their feet and so, with a heavy heart, I have decided to dispense with your services as Lead Singer. Please understand that this is a business decision and not personal at all.

Nicola stared at the screen.

It was a joke. Surely, it was just a joke. He couldn't seriously be firing her! If the band had won, it would largely have been because of her performance. That wasn't ego talking – it was a simple fact that bands were remembered more for their singers than anything else.

So, did this mean that the promoters didn't like her? Did they say they'd take the band but only without her? Doubts suddenly crowded into Nicola's mind. Had she done something wrong? She knew that her performance had been good – she had honestly thought it was perfect – so it couldn't be that. Could it?

She read the text again. No, that wasn't it. *I have decided... I feel... a business decision...* No, this was all Mike. He was removing her. But why...?

And suddenly something that had been at the back of her mind for days leapt forward.

The girl in the Subway station. The girl she had seen Mike with. She knew her.

Her name was Gerri, or Jinny, or... Gina! That was it. Gina. Nicola had seen her perform. Months ago, at a showcase that they had both been involved in. She wasn't great, but she had something. Her voice was fine, nothing special, but she had known how to dress for the male judges, known how to sell what she had.

Even so, she didn't think that Gina would be conniving enough to get Nicola replaced. This had to be all about Mike. Whether he was trying to impress his girlfriend or just keep her, the decision had been his. Not fucking personal, eh!

Nicola threw her phone across the room. It made a small dent in the wall on impact and, as it hit the floor, Nicola felt her legs give way beneath her. Curled up in the middle of her room, she cried herself into unconsciousness.

Paul brought her coffee over and Nicola thanked him.

"Least I could do, really," he said, and she noticed that, for the first time since they'd met in the coffee shop, he couldn't meet her eyes.

"I don't blame you," she said. "You've got to look after yourself in this business. I wasn't expecting you to leave when I forwarded Mike's text. I just wanted you all to know what a bastard he was."

Paul nodded. "I did think about it," he said. "We all did. Davey especially was very vocal about it."

Nicola smiled at the silent drummer having finally found his voice.

"But in the end, we just couldn't afford it. You know how it is, Nic."

She did. In the three weeks since that night, one week since the concerts at the SECC, Nicola had done a lot of thinking. She had even resolved herself to the fact that, if the positions had been reversed, if one of the other band members had been replaced, she would probably have stayed too. She wasn't very keen on what it said about her, but she was honest enough to admit it.

"So how did it go?"

Paul put down his drink and looked straight at her. "Look, I just want to say, she's not you. She's not got your range, or your talent. She's definitely not got your personality, on stage or off."

"Thank you," Nicola said. "But..."

"But she did a good job up there. I'm not saying you wouldn't have done it better, you would have, but for what we needed, she was okay. And Mike says we have had a few rumblings from a label as a result. Not one of the majors, but enough to get a deal out of it."

"I'm pleased for you," Nicola said, and was surprised to realise that she actually meant it.

"Mind you, though" Paul continued, looking around them quickly before speaking, "I don't know how long she'll be with Mike after this. On the first night, Keith saw the headliner talking to her. He seemed to be very cosy. By the last show, she'd graduated to a private after-show party with him. And Mike wasn't invited!"

It was like spying on a parallel world, Nicola thought. If she'd been there, would she have taken the star up on his advances? She'd like to think not, but in the excitement of the evening, with 13,000 people chanting his name and him only wanting to say yours, would it have been so clear?

"Well, they do say all good things come to those who wait – but I have to admit I thought I'd have to wait a bit longer to see Mike get his," she said.

Paul smiled. "So, er, what are you up to?" he asked. It was good of him to enquire – they both knew she wouldn't have anywhere near as big news as his.

"Same old, same old," Nicola replied. "You pick yourself up and dust yourself off and just get on with things."

"And spout a lot of platitudes, too," said Paul, giving her another of his Dad Looks. "Seriously, Nic. How are you?"

What could she say? That she had spent a week just being angry, taking her frustration out on anyone who came near her? That, for the first time ever, she had cancelled a paying gig just because she didn't have the confidence to do it? That there were days still where she would suddenly find herself crying? Or that in the end she'd come to realise that nothing lasts – not happiness, certainly not fame, not even depression - because she had clawed herself back out of that pit and was now, singing again.

"I'm good," she said. "I've learned a lot. About people and about me. But I've got a gig this weekend, just a wedding but it sounds a good one, and I might have found an R&B and soul band that need a singer, so I'm moving on."

It was true. Somehow, the whole affair with Mike had put things into perspective for her.

Nicola took a swig of her coffee. "I'm going to get through this, Paul, I'm going to focus more on my material" she said, giving him a wink. "And you watch - I'm going to be even bigger than The Moneymakers!"

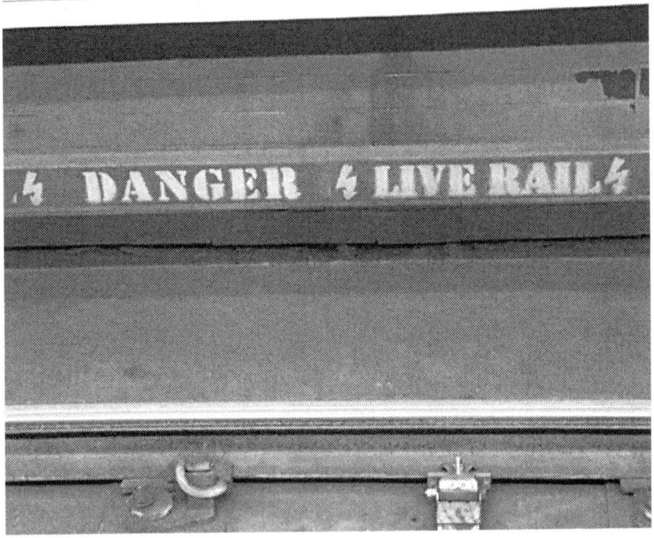
DANGER
LIVE RAIL

Govan to **St George's Cross**

"Why are there nae Scottish superheroes?"

Jag took a moment to think about it. "Well, there must be. I mean, there's..."

"Aye," said Robbie. "Go on. Ah'll wait."

Jag continued his musing as they waited for the train to arrive. It was important stuff.

"Well, there's the X-Men," he said in the end. "I mean, there's hunners a' them. Summa them must be Scottish."

"Can't think of enny," Robbie replied, and Jag knew his friend would be the one to know if there was. He practically lived in Forbidden Planet on Sauchiehall Street.

"And ye can't help thinking, they've missed a trick there," he continued. "Ah mean, there's a fuckin' X right there on tha Scottish flag!"

"Aye," Jag decided to run with it. "You could call 'em The Saltire Squad! They could be a little sub-team, used for missions over the Border the noo."

Robbie grinned. "Saltire Squad Forever! And you'd have heroes with special Scottish powers."

There was a moment's silence. Jag glanced up at the arrivals sign - 3 minutes till the next train on the Inner Line.

"There'd be Muckle Coo, a great hairy bugger wi' the strength of ten men," Robbie said. "But only if he had enough alcohol in his system."

Jag grinned. "And there'd be another who could control the weather, so there would. But only driving rain and a biting fuckin' wind! An' his name would be..."

The two looked at each other for a moment.

"Pish!" Robbie said, and the two laughed. "Aye - beware the power of Pish!"

The two friends laughed some more.

"And there'd be one who everything he touched would become deep fried! Deep fried and a weapon. He'd be cutting folk down wi' throwing crusty pizzas at the buggers!"

Robbie was on a roll now. Jag knew better than to interrupt. It was far more fun to just let him freewheel his way into a fantasy world.

"He'd be a big fat guy and he'd be called Fryer Fuck! And his best friend would be on the team too, a scrawny little bugger whose power would be to turn intae a cloud of fuckin' midges to attack villains."

Robbie looked up from his reverie and winked at his lifelong friend.

"An' his name would be Wee Bitey Bastard."

The two of them laughed out loud, so loud that they drew the attention of other passengers waiting further down the platform. One of them gave them a disapproving look.

"Ah, whit ye lookin' at, you smug bastard?" Robbie shouted. "Do ye not know what fun is? Nah, I bet ye don't."

The man looked away and Jag tried to pull his friend back from the temper that had just surged.

"Aye, that's great, it is," he said. "But they're gunna need some villains to fight."

"That's easy," Robbie replied. "That's the League A' Tory Bastards outta Westminster." But his face was hard now and the joy of a few seconds earlier was gone.

Jag was about to say more but a sudden cold wind on their backs signalled that the train was approaching.

Further conversation was impossible in the train. The lads sat opposite one another at the far end of the carriage, on the small double seats just before the door through to the next coach. These were prized seats - although there was room for someone to sit next to you, a lone woman never would and a bloke would never voluntarily sit that close to another guy he didn't know. As a result, anyone occupying these seats got the space to spread out as much as they wanted.

The downside to this was that it also seemed to be the noisiest part of the train. The roar of the wheels going over the tracks, the banshee scream of the brakes, all echoing off the walls of the subway tunnels made sure the two passed their journey in silence.

Jag took the opportunity to study his friend.

The two had known each other since the first year of Secondary School. He couldn't remember how they had met but somehow the boys had just gravitated towards one another, bonding over a shared love of comic books and a mutual dislike of football practice.

Now, ten years later, they were still the best of pals. They'd seen girlfriends come and go, weathered the trials and disappointments of exams, and were now both working in separate branches of the same store. Their lives were completely intertwined.

And yet...

As he looked across at the chunky, dark-haired and unshaven guy across from him, Jag was aware that things between them were starting to change.

Jag worked at the Poundland on Great Western Road. He'd been there for two years and had been instrumental in getting Robbie his job at the Sauchiehall Street branch. Prior to that, Robbie had never seemed to have any luck with employment. He'd had several jobs since school, but nothing had seemed to stick. Employment for Robbie usually ended with him walking out, loudly complaining about 'wee small-minded fucks' or stupidly rigid regulations.

Naturally, Jag had wanted his friend to find a decent job and Robbie had seemed interested in Poundland whenever the two talked about it. So, Jag had told him about the vacancy when it came up, coached him for the interview and even put in a good word with the then-manager of the store. It had been a walk-over.

And, for a few months, it had been great – the two of them swapping war stories about customers, sharing complaints about stock, picking out which female colleagues were the fittest.

Then the rumours had started. Jag first heard talk about an 'awkward' staff member through a colleague from another branch. There had been an argument between co-workers, the story went, one that had threatened to spill out onto the store floor, and one staff member in particular was on the brink of being disciplined because of it. There was even talk of someone having had a packet of super-soft toilet rolls thrown at them. The whole story had been relayed to him in a jovial, tales-behind-the-bikeshed way and Jag had thought nothing much of it beyond vowing to ask Robbie if he knew who this unruly colleague was when they next met.

Before he could, however, another story started to make the rounds. He heard this one from a colleague who knew both the lads, and this time it was obvious that Robbie wouldn't just know about it - Robbie was the problem.

"He was arguing with Rollo," the friend had said. Rollo was the Assistant Manager of the Sauchiehall Street store. "Proper stand-up row. I mean, it was in the stock area, but only because Rollo took it back there. And Jennifer said you could hear some of it in the store."

Jag hadn't found out at the time what the cause of the argument had been, but he learned all about it the next day from Robbie.

"Fuckin' arsehole!" he'd said. "That Rollo prick. Wanted me tae take down a display I'd put up the day before and rebuild the thing two aisles over! He claimed he'd told me it should be there in the first place, but he didnae! Tryin' a cover for his own piss up."

"Was it a big job?" Jag had asked.

"Nah," his friend replied. "Wouldnae have taken quarter of an 'oor, but I hadna done it wrong in the first place!"

Jag had made sympathetic noises, saying that it was just the way it was and Rollo was just flexing his manager's muscles, but in truth he'd never heard a bad word against the Assistant Manager. He was generally well liked by everyone.

Thankfully, after that, things seemed to calm down. There were occasional reports back that Robbie could be abrasive with colleagues, or that he had been spoken to about his language on the store floor, but on the whole, he seemed to be settling into the job and Jag told himself that the earlier problems had just been teething troubles.

However, it wasn't quite as easy to ignore the changes in Robbie outside the store.

Robbie had always had a temper. At school, he'd been happier to let his fists fly rather than argue his way out of a situation. This had been a good and a bad thing as far as Jag was concerned – quite often those fists had flown as Robbie protected his thinner, less imposing friend from bullies, but it had also led both boys into a lot of trouble with their teachers.

When they had left school, the anger had seemed to drain out of Robbie for a while. Left to their own devices, enjoying an extended summer break (in their eyes), the two had bummed around town, enjoying afternoons on Glasgow Green with a tinnie or evenings down the pub. Strangely, alcohol always seemed to have a calming effect on Robbie. Jag had known guys who turned into complete wankers after a few pints and wanted to pick a fight with anyone near them, but Robbie just seemed to mellow as the drink flowed and he'd even been known to walk away from a fight at the end of a good session.

Which was great – except once they started work, Robbie spent more time sober than he did drunk.

And his temper was definitely back. It showed in his attitude to work but it also flared up in the most unlikely of places. Only the week before, Robbie had kicked off in a fish and chippie because they were out of haggis pakoras. It had been a good night until that point, and the rage had appeared out of nowhere. As he had pulled him out of the shop and away from the irate server, Jag realised that, after years of having Robbie protect him, he was now in the position of having to protect his friend. From himself.

The train pulled in at St George's Cross and the two of them got off.

"It's like a bloody maze in 'ere", Robbie said as they headed for the escalators, no trace of his earlier ill-temper in his voice. The route to the surface was not as direct as in some stations, but Jag stayed quiet about it.

As they came out into the fresh October air, Robbie turned to his pal. "So, where's this shop?"

"It's not one shop," Jag started to explain. They were here to walk up Great Western Road and scout out the many charity shops that lay along it in the hope that they could find decent costumes for Halloween. "There's plenty to choose from round here."

"Wull, I'll take your word for it," his friend replied. "Ah've nae been here before. Which way?"

The exit from the station was a little confusing. The two had emerged into a concrete corridor which split into two ramps ahead of them. There were signs but they couldn't see any roads or buildings above the walls.

"This way," Jag said confidently.

They emerged from the Subway station onto a main road. Behind them, Great Western Road could be seen, stretching away on a curve of promise. There were a few other shops just ahead of them, and a traffic island that seemed to have been made into a small park.

"Let's start there," Robbie said, striding out across the road, seemingly without checking for traffic. Jag was about to say that there wasn't a lot of point, that there were no charity shops there, but he decided against it.

His friend was in a good mood and enthusiastic about their trip. It might not last. Better to go with the flow.

"Well, I can see why they called it St George's Cross," Robbie said, "but why tha fuck have we got that English prick in Scotland?"

The two of them were looking up at the statue at one end of the traffic island. It depicted a knight on horseback in the midst of stabbing a dragon lying at the base of the sculpture. The lance he presumably would have used was long since gone.

"Sez here it was given to the people of Glasgow by the Co-operative Society," Jag read from the plaque on the plinth.

"They can bloody keep it," his friend declared. "Still doesn't answer the question."

"There was a St George's Church, er, somewhere round here," Jag tried. "Perhaps it was connected to that."

The two of them continued to study the statue. It seemed very out of place on a traffic island, even without the nationalistic connotations. A rather ornate wrought iron fence surrounded it, presumably to stop people climbing up on the saint's back. Although why they'd want to Jag wasn't sure - mildew and bird lime covered every inch of it.

"Doesnae look like a very scary dragon," Jag said, hoping to break his friend's interest in the tableau. "The horse is bigger."

"Mebbe it's a wain," Robbie suggested. "Just like the English to skewer a poor wee babby. Probably told everyone back home it was the size of a bus."

For as long as he had known him, Jag had wondered where Robbie's hatred of the English came from. It didn't seem to be a political thing. Robbie's hatred pre-dated the lads' understanding of Independence and his parents didn't seem to hold the same views, so it was a bit of a mystery. Whatever the cause, it at least gave his friend an imaginary enemy to rail against.

"Ennyway, we should be gettin' off," Jag said. "My costume isnae gunna find itself."

Robbie didn't seem to hear him. He just stared at the statue.

Jag started to say his name, but his friend suddenly lurched forward. The railings surrounding the statue were pointed, like ornate arrowheads, but the corner posts were rounded and it was one of these that Robbie made a grab for. One of the arrowheads further along was missing so he swung his leg up and placed his foot there. With effort, Robbie was able to stand, precariously, on a level with the bottom of the statue.

"Whit you doin'?", Jag shouted, looking around frantically in case they were seen. Robbie grinned down at him.

"Get yer camera oot," he said. "I'm goin' climbing."

Steadying himself with one hand on the corner post, Robbie once more swung his leg out to put it on the statue's base. St George looked down on him quizzically. However, the plinth he stood on was both higher up and further away than Robbie had anticipated, and his foot slipped on the mildew covering it. With a slight cry, Robbie slipped off both the statue and the railings and landed in a tangled heap between the two.

Jag rushed forwards. "Are ye alright?"

To his surprise, Robbie was laughing. There wasn't a lot of room between the railings and the stone, certainly not enough to fit a man the size of Robbie with ease, and as a result he was crammed awkwardly into the space; one foot on the ground, one level with the railings, one hand still grasping the corner post. He reminded Jag of when you find a dead spider, all twisted and curled up.

"Fuckin' English," Robbie said, but with a wink. "Always puttin' us doon."

"Come 'ere," Jag said, extending a hand over the railings. "Let's get you out."

Before he could grab his friend, however, a voice boomed out behind him.

"What the hell are you two doing?"

Jag turned around, fearing it was the police, but instead a short, round, red-faced man was approaching them. He was in shirtsleeves despite the cold, suggesting that he had come from one of the nearby flats or shops.

"It's alright," Jag began. "We were just on oor way."

"I've called the police," the man said, pulling to a stop in front of Jag. "I've had enough of you neds trying to climb that thing. Or sitting around here smoking weed."

"Hey, hey!" Jag raised his hands to calm the man. "We've never been here before the noo! Yeah, it wuz a daft thing to do, fair play, but we're movin' on. Nae need to involve the Polis."

The man waved his arguments aside. "They'll be here soon," he said. "You've smoked your last joint here."

"Look, ye're no listening," Jag tried. "We're no staying and we've never been here before. Ye can get the Polis here if you want, but we'll be gone – and we'll take our imaginary joints wi' us!"

The man got even more red faced at this reply and jabbed a finger into Jag's chest. "You'll stay here," he said.

Jag was about to reply when suddenly another hand shot out and grabbed the man's finger. Robbie had managed to climb out from behind the railings.

"You dinnae talk to us like that, ye wee streak a' pish," he said as he stepped around his friend. Robbie was the taller of the two anyway, and he now towered over the irate man.

"Rob, it's okay," Jag began, but it was too late. Robbie had tight hold of the man's hand and was starting to bend his finger back. The man sank to his knees.

"You can't, you can't…" he stuttered, but Robbie continued to apply pressure to his finger. The man cried out in pain.

Jag watched as if in a trance. The shock of Robbie having appeared, followed by the violence of his actions made it feel as if he was watching a film rather than real events. He felt distanced from the scene playing out before him. Even when he clearly heard the man's finger snap, his mind said that it couldn't have been Robbie who was responsible. It must be someone else, an actor. The furious person stood before him, face twisted in a rage Jag had never seen before, couldn't be his friend.

The man was curled up on the ground now, howling in pain. Still it didn't seem real to Jag.

And then the Robbie-actor stepped forward and kicked the man hard in the stomach. The man retched and threw up on the pavement. The smell of vomit was suddenly acrid in the air.

But you can't smell things in a film, Jag thought.

The small man coughed, a wet, hacking sound, and suddenly Jag snapped out of his reverie. It was happening. It was real.

He looked over at the attacker who was quite clearly his friend. Naked aggression was written all over his face, his body tense with fury. Robbie was crouching down slightly, one arm drawn back as he prepared to punch the pitiful figure on the floor.

Jag knew that if he didn't do something, Robbie might actually kill the man. He reached out and grabbed Robbie by the shoulder to pull him back.

"We need to go," he started to say, but before the thought had become words Robbie pivoted around and punched him hard in the face.

Time stopped.

Jag felt the punch but not the pain, just a force pushing him back. He saw his friend staring at him, the realisation of what he had done growing in his eyes. He saw the man unmoving on the ground.

Then everything started again and the pain in his jaw crashed in. He felt a tooth move in his mouth and tasted blood. The railings around the statue suddenly slammed into his back, hard and unyielding.

Jag slumped to the floor. He spat blood out, aiming for the pavement but just soiling his jacket instead. Robbie was looking at him, horror on his face.

"I didnae mean, I didnae know..." he stumbled over the words. He held a hand out. Jag batted it away.

"Fuck off," he said. Robbie stared at him.

"Ah mean it, fuck off!" Jag said, louder. "Just go!"

Robbie continued to stare at him for a beat and then, without even a glance at the man behind him, ran off.

The Polis eventually arrived, two beat cops who had been in the area. It turned out that the angry man had been bluffing originally, but one of the local shopkeepers called them after spotting the fight outside. Jag was still sat beneath the vanquished dragon when they showed up.

Waiting had given him time to think. In some ways, he acknowledged that this moment had been coming for some time. Robbie had always been quick to anger, often irrationally so, and it was only a matter of time before Jag would have been the recipient of it. The Robbie he had grown up with was no longer the same one he knew today and even friendship might not be able to withstand his growing anger.

Yet friendship was what bound them, and Jag knew that he wasn't ready to give up on that just yet. Robbie needed help. Professional help. If he told the police the name of the attacker, would he be able to get his friend that help?

Possibly. But Robbie would also lose his job and get a criminal record that would likely bar him from another. And, of course, there was the possibility that he would go to jail. Jag knew that he had a man's entire life in his hands and a nagging question in his head – could this, *would* this, happen again?

Throughout his thoughts, he kept coming back to that eternal moment after the punch had landed. Seeing the realisation in Robbie's eyes of what he had done. What, he wondered, had his friend seen in Jag's eyes? Shock? Hurt? Betrayal?

At first, the police were more concerned with the man Robbie had attacked than with him. An ambulance arrived and the man was taken away, the paramedics also giving Jag a quick look over before they departed. Then it was time for the questions.

A stocky cop who looked like he only just fitted into his protective vest helped Jag to his feet and confirmed his name from their initial contact on arrival.

"And do you know the name of the person responsible for this attack?" he asked, notebook poised.

Jag lifted his head, unsure even then of what his answer would be.

Behind the cop, the second Polis was trying to turn a small crowd away. One tall figure was trying to push their way forward all the same.

Jag shook his head to clear it. "Sorry," he said. "Still a bit groggy."

"That's alright, sir," the cop said. "In your own time."

Jag opened his mouth to speak but the crackle of the cop's radio cut in. He listened for a moment, then excused himself and went over to his colleague. Jag watched disinterestedly, his thoughts still in turmoil.

It seemed the tall figure had made their way to the front of the group and was now talking with the second cop. It was only when the cop moved to one side briefly that Jag could see that the figure was Robbie.

The first cop stepped in and brought Robbie over to Jag, one hand firmly holding the young man's arm. Robbie was back to his usual self, no anger visible. If anything, he looked more at peace than Jag had seen him for a long time.

"This gentleman has come forward to say that he was the attacker. Can you corroborate this claim?"

Jag looked into the eyes of his friend.

"It's okay," Robbie said. "This isn't a decision you should have tae make."

Jag looked at him for a moment longer, then turned his attention to the cop and nodded. "Aye, this is the guy."

Robbie winked at his friend. Both knew that their friendship was about to change, but they also knew that it was still there.

Jag gave his friend a last smile before the polis led him away.

"Saltire Squad Forever," he said.

If you see anything suspicious, report it to our staff or the Police immediately.

Kelvinbridge to West Street

I'm the guy who sits beside you on the train and reads your Metro newspaper through sideways glances.

I don't do it every day. Some days I position myself so that I can just look at the back of your neck, where your soft brown hair curls slightly and flows over your collar. I like that – it's a part of yourself that even you can't see. It's special to me.

I like observing you. Sometimes, when you take that large bag into work, the one that won't close properly because you have too much stuff in it, I try to see what it is that swells it so. To see what is important to you.

If you are reading this now, it means that you have had that bag with you today, because I intend to drop this note into it for you to find. Please don't be alarmed by it – I mean no harm. This letter is here to help you, to let you know the danger you are in. Not from me. I would never hurt you. It's him you have to worry about.

I just want you to know that I am here. That you are being looked after. I suppose you could say it's a love letter.

I started watching you two years ago.

I was going through a bad patch in my life. My job was boring me to tears and hardly bringing in enough money to live on. I had a girlfriend, Karen, but we were growing apart. Every night, I came home and the house felt that little bit quieter, as if she was leaving me by degrees. There was nothing that I could put my finger on, but Karen was gradually removing herself from my life and I couldn't really be bothered to do anything about it.

I suppose part of the problem between Karen and me was that I am so boring. There's no need to say that I'm not - after all, you don't even know who I am. I always have been boring. At school, I was the kid who made friends easily enough but who preferred his own company; the one who was good enough at games and clever enough in his lessons to attract neither praise nor censorship. I was neither brilliant nor stupid, a bully nor bullied. I dare say if you went back to my class now and asked anyone about me, they'd find it difficult to remember me at all. I was the grey boy who became the grey man. Quiet, unobtrusive, unknown. Average.

There are plenty like me in life. We are the ones who oil the wheels for those who lead the exciting lives. We provide the infrastructure to your adventures. We don't participate; we watch. And once I realised that, I was okay.

It became a habit of mine, watching. I found that it was a feature of being grey that you could stand anywhere, any busy place or half empty corridor, anywhere where people would expect to see you anyway, and you could watch without being seen. It was like a special kind of invisibility. When people attach no importance to you, you are free to do whatever you like. There is liberation in greyness.

At first, I just watched everyone indiscriminately. It was amusing to note the shifting patterns that crowds made. Take standing at a subway station, for example. The commuter run in a morning – I know you're familiar with that. All you see, if you look at all, is a bunch of people stood around, waiting for a train. Their positions are random, their moods hidden. But I see something totally different.

Over time, you notice that the positioning of everyone is exact. Seasoned commuters have their own spots to stand in. They walk up, reading the newspaper or glancing at their shoes (never at each other), and take their territory. The prize places are where the train doors will open. I see them judging how close to the edge of the platform they can stand to be able to let people off the train without sacrificing that important first place. It's quite amusing really.

And, once you realise that their patterns are not your patterns, you see a lot more.

Anyway, that was how it started. And when I got onto the train it was no different. Still no one saw me, but I was free to look at all of them.

You were not the first person I watched. That was a young man, all gangly arms and swagger, who usually got into the carriage last and stood up for the whole journey. He didn't get on at your stop, so you might not have seen him. He stood by the doors, leaning against the walls and listening to one of those music player things that they have. I don't know what the music was – something with tinny beats that seemed to go far too fast – but he listened to it a lot. Every morning. Sometimes so loud that other people stood around him could hear it too.

I first watched him from a seat further down the carriage. I don't know why he caught my attention. Perhaps it was because, out of all the other passengers there, he was the one most securely in another world. He was in the music. He listened to it on the platform (I learned later that he listened to it on his walk to and from the station too), and he listened to it on the train. Hermetically sealed against the day. I suppose that he was the mirror image of me, if I think about it. We both stood apart from the other travellers, but whereas he looked inside himself, I looked out at them.

One day, I tried to hear what he was listening to. I decided before we arrived at his station that I would give up my seat and go and stand in the doorway to wait for him. I remember that an old lady got my seat and I was pleased that my actions had done good for others as well. When we got to his station, he was waiting in the same place as usual, and he got onto the train and stood by me without giving it a thought.

But I was electrified. I could have reached out and touched him. I could have plucked one of those headphones out of his ears and heard precisely what he was listening to, at the same time as he was hearing it through the remaining headphone. I was so close as to be able to smell him. Yet I did nothing. I knew that to do anything other than to stand there, to be grey by his side, would break the spell. He would notice me, and then I could no longer watch him.

And it was at that point, when I realised that I had gone as far with him as I could, that you walked into my life.

You won't remember it. All you did was get on the train at Kelvinbridge and take a seat that some gentleman gave up for you. It was a normal day for you, the actions no more special than breathing. But you were sat facing me – not looking, just facing – and therefore I could look at you with ease.

You are beautiful, you know. I know that boyfriends will tell you that, but you expect them to. I say it because it is true. The way your hair frames your face, the delicate curve of your jaw line, the surprise of your green eyes – all these things set you apart from other women. I daresay you had been a passenger on that train many times before, but then, at that time, you became obvious to me. I suppose it was because I was in a different place. Really, I ought to thank the boy for bringing us together.

But, of course, I can't do that.

Anyway, from that day, I began to watch you. Taking my cue from that first meeting, I started to vary my seating positions. Some days I would sit opposite you; on others, I would be just a bit further along the carriage. I could be on the same side as you or opposite, it didn't matter – I seemed to instinctively know where you were. Back then, I never sat on the seat next to you. I didn't want this experience to end as I thought it had done with the boy. Sometimes, though, I would sit close enough to reach out and touch you. I played a game with myself at times like that. I would try to see how much of you I could see without becoming noticeable. I could, for example, have just turned my head and stared at you, taking in all the details of your clothes, your posture, your makeup, but I didn't do that. I knew that I had to watch you from outside the pattern of your life. I couldn't join it; I could only observe.

So, I learned to see you from the corner of my eyes. I dropped my newspaper (not too often, as that in itself would mark me out) and was able to steal a look at the slender grace of your legs as I picked it up. I pretended to search for something in the inside pocket of my jacket and was able to secretly gaze at you over the top of my lapel. One wonderful morning, when you had an uncharacteristic sneezing fit, I even managed to hand you a paper handkerchief that I had in my pocket. It was a wonderful moment – finally, I was able to look at you fully without causing suspicion.

I suppose it was really only a game with me, something to pass the time. Some days, I would even sit in another part of the carriage completely, knowing that from this position I would not be able to see you. Knowing you were there but that I was deliberately ignoring you (yet not – you were constantly in my thoughts on these occasions) was a most delicious feeling.

Then there came the time you went away.

It was last summer. I had been watching you for about six months by then, every morning choosing my seat on the train with care and precision so as to observe a new facet of your beauty. This particular morning, I had chosen a seat that was very close to where you usually sat, one where I could see you face on. And, as usual, as we pulled in to Kelvinbridge, I had that frisson of pleasure, that tingle of expectation, that presaged your arrival. But you were not there.

Instead, some old woman, all white hair and pearls, sat in your place. I could not believe it. I scanned the carriage for a sign of you, to see if you had sat somewhere else, but I could not see you. I even abandoned my own seat and walked to the far end of the carriage so as to see everyone in it. You were not there.

As we pulled in at St George's Cross, I hurriedly left the carriage and pushed my way through the morning crowds to get into the next one, thinking perhaps you had got onto the wrong coach by mistake. But you were not there either. I went through as many coaches as I could before your usual last stop, searching every face, looking at every seat, but the truth of it was you had not got onto the train.

By the time we reached West Street, I was beside myself. What had started as concern had changed to panic, and beyond that I could sense fear waiting to pounce. I stood on that unfamiliar platform, watching the other passengers stream past me until I was sure you were not amongst them, and I felt my life crumble. You had become the focus of my mornings. I needed you. Without you, I was just grey again; the patterns made no sense.

I found it difficult to concentrate at work that day, and in the evening I hardly slept. When morning came, I rose and shaved far earlier than I normally would, and then waited, impatient and nervous, until the time I could go out for our train. But when I did catch it, when I reached your station, you were not there again.

I couldn't understand it. I thought perhaps I had done something wrong, that I had got the carriage wrong for some reason, or that you had seen me and were deliberately avoiding your usual seat. A thousand scenarios ran through my head, all of them my fault.

The week ended and still you had not returned. I spent the weekend planning what to do if you did not reappear on Monday. I did not sleep well. I had very little appetite. I could not even be bothered to talk to Karen and we spent those two days in stilted silence. It was a few weeks after this that she told me she was leaving, but if she had said it that weekend I doubt if I would even have heard her.

Monday came, and I climbed aboard the subway train with sweaty hands and a cold chill through my body. The journey to Kelvinbridge took an age. I had positioned myself by the central doors, so that I could see everyone who got on, and I watched each person intently as they wandered into the carriage and took their seats.

You were not amongst them.

I got off at the next station in a panic and, having somehow made my way to the surface, rang into work. I was ill, I told them. I couldn't possibly come in. I needed to see a doctor and I expected I would have to take the week off. They made sympathetic noises in return, but I could tell that I was no great loss to them. I was a drone and other drones would fill my space for the moment. I doubted if most of them would even notice I was missing.

Then I boarded the next train and went back to Kelvinbridge.

It was unusual being there, standing in places that you must have stood. I don't quite know why I went. I knew there would have been no physical evidence of your having been there, no perfume on the breeze, no dropped handkerchief on the platform, but all the same I needed to go. I spent an hour on the platform, my mind following phantom versions of you as they wandered about it, only leaving when the Subway staff – evidently having noticed me on the CCTV – came down to make sure I was alright. I made some kind of dazed excuse and left.

The next day, I got up early and caught the train to Kelvinbridge again. I was on your platform an hour before your usual arrival time. I sat on a bench and watched the commuters arriving. I studied their patterns and noticed how similar they were to those of my own station's travellers. I watched the dance repeat itself as train after train pulled in. And I waited for you, but you never came.

I waited for a further two hours after your usual train had left, and then I thought about it again. The next day, I was back on your platform, once again an hour early, but now further along the track. I thought that you might be getting on at a different part of the train, but you were not there then either. Nor were you there the next day, when I waited at the other end of the platform. And on the final day, when I stood on the platform opposite yours, now not caring if you saw me scanning the lines of bored morning faces, you still were not there.

I returned home and spent a wretched weekend wondering what it was that I had done to send you away.

Monday came around again, but I had no interest in it. I took my place in the ranks of the grey at the station and chose an arbitrary seat on the train when it arrived. I had no reason to care where I sat anymore. We pulled in to Kelvinbridge and I hardly even glanced up.

But as we pulled out, I did lift my head, and as I did, so meaning and colour came back to my world. You were there. Sitting not two seats away, your head down slightly as you searched through your bag for something. At first, I wasn't even sure it was you – I wasn't ready to believe you had returned to me – but then you looked up and I saw you clearly. You were more beautiful than ever, your hair shining in the morning light, your skin even more tanned and healthy than usual.

I felt as if I had done penance for some unknown sin but had now been forgiven. It was as if God himself had smiled upon me.

You looked over in my direction and I looked down sharply, eager not to cause offence again. As I did this, I saw a dark stain on the crotch of my trousers and realised that I had been so excited by your return that I had wet myself.

After losing you, I realised I never wanted to go through that uncertainty again. It was no good just seeing you on the train anymore – the pattern was too small, too fragile. I needed to know more about you.

I had never seen you on the train going home. I don't know if we left at different times, or if I had just not looked for you, content in my morning sightings. Now, however, I wanted to see you on that journey too. But how?

The easiest way was to find out where you worked. So, one morning, after I had arranged to arrive late to my own work, I followed you. I got off at West Street with you and made my way to the surface content that I was hidden amongst all the other passengers who alighted there. And then I walked up to your office and found out who you are.

It's funny, but I had expected you to be something in Marketing, some high flyer with minions and accounts. So, when you first turned into that District Council building, I thought you must have been visiting a client there and I cursed myself for not seeing this eventuality. But, as I watched you through the glass doors, I saw you wave to the Receptionist and walk through the foyer as if it was something you did every day, and I knew then that you worked there.

It didn't matter. I thought no less of you, but it was a surprise.

Yet I was only halfway there. As soon as you had got into the elevator and the doors had closed, I entered the building myself. I knew what I was doing; I had thought it through many times. I asked the receptionist who you were. Of course, it was not that blatant – I made up a story about having seen you outside and the astonishing resemblance you had to an old school friend of mine. I even gave this fictional acquaintance's name, and, as expected, the receptionist corrected me.

And now I knew you. I have to say, you do have a beautiful name. Lilting and musical, a fitting epithet for so sweet a person. It trips off my tongue with ease and pleasure. I can say it hundreds of times and still never tire of it.

Having succeeded so far, however, I returned to my work with a spring in my step, resolving to do no more that day. It was another game, you see, another pattern to uncover. No need to rush it.

Three days later, I rang your office and asked to make an appointment with you. The secretary who answered was perfectly happy to do this until I told her I was working until six and could not come to your offices until after that time. That was difficult, she said, because you left work at five.

And there I had it. A quick check of the timetables and I knew which subway train you would be catching home. Even so, I left it for another week before I tested my theory out. Oh, that time stretched out in front of me so tantalisingly, but I was determined not to act until I felt the time was right.

I waited for you at the West Street station, and you came. On time, as expected, and with this act, so the pattern of your life became clearer.

Now I varied the times that I watched you. Sometimes I would wait for you on the morning train as usual, but occasionally I would deliberately get into the wrong carriage, certain that I would instead see you in the evening. In some ways, the anticipation present throughout those days was the most exciting thing about our meetings. I would try to work, but all the time my mind would be wondering what you would be wearing that day. The rose pink skirt or the blue one? The green pumps or the black heels? The expectation was most distracting.

And, on the mornings when I did not look for you, I resumed watching the young man with the music. For some reason, this felt right. I had dismissed him too early and, now that I knew the possibilities inherent in our situation, now that you had shown me that we could be more than merely strangers, I felt the need to return to him.

It was the young man who gave me the idea of where to go next. I had travelled into work that morning with you and was expecting a quiet journey home on my own. Yet, shortly after I had sat down, I became aware of a tinny noise nearby. At first, I tried to ignore it, but after a while I realised what it might be. I hardly dared to hope really, but nonetheless I turned in my seat to find the source of the noise.

It was indeed my young man, sat only two seats beyond me. His eyes were closed and his fingers tapped out a frantic rhythm on the knees of his jeans, oblivious to everyone else. There was a businessman sat next to him and he threw the young man the occasional sharp look, but it had no effect.

I sat back in my seat and smiled. I remember feeling happy that he was there, that another part of the pattern was falling into place. I didn't know what it was as then, but I could feel the pieces beginning to merge, feel order approaching from coincidence.

When the young man got off at his station, I was only mildly surprised to see that I had done so too. I have no memory of getting up or leaving the train. I was just there, standing on the platform, watching him wander off ahead of me with his music playing in his head.

And, of course, I followed him.

Once I had your name, it was easy to find out more about you. The internet and social media are wonderful things.

After only a small search, I was able to take a trip out to where you live, while you were at work. I didn't try to go in – Good Heavens, I couldn't invade your privacy like that! – but I could look. I could see the sort of flat you had, and luckily it was on the ground floor, so I could see at least some of your life through the windows. And I was able to tell that you lived alone and that made my heart sing with the possibilities for the two of us.

For, now that I knew more about you, I could see how compatible we were. I know that, reading this, you might not see how that can be, but it is. In fact, I think that you and I are destined to be together. And I thought that even more after I first saw him.

But I am getting ahead of myself. He didn't notice you for some time yet.

It was the young man he saw first.

I continued my usual watching after I found out who you were, content in knowing what I did, in being the secret admirer. There was no need for me to do more. I still saw the young man too. I had decided that he was a sort of unwitting muse for me. Time and again he had shown me where to go, how to see the patterns more clearly. And he did not disappoint this time, although it took me a while to realise.

For example, I can't remember when it was that I realised someone else was watching him too. It sort of sneaked up on me. I had seen a man in a grey raincoat standing by him one day and thought nothing of him. He was a grey person too and I fell into the trap. The raincoat was even the same as mine.

Yet eventually it dawned on me. It was nothing that your average commuter would see. To them, the movements of their fellow passengers were either dull monotony or acts of confusion, but I saw beyond that. I started to see the new pattern.

He was very careful not to be seen. Sometimes it was only a reflection in a window that gave him away. A half-caught movement. But to me it was obvious. For a short while, I'll admit, I even stopped watching you. There was a fascination in this new scenario, like watching a game being played when both competitors were unaware of their audience and only one of them knew the rules. I needed to know what was going on. I needed to see who this other watcher was.

And then, one day, I saw the young man get off at his station and as the train pulled away, as the crowd milled around to get to the escalators, I saw a flash of grey, a familiar coat surfacing like a fin in a sea of people, and I knew that the watcher had got off the train with him. I stared out of the window as the train slid out of the station and into the tunnels, and I knew that I would never see the young man again. I knew it.

Two weeks later, I realised the man was now watching you.

I had been upset by the loss of the young man. I looked out for him every morning, but he never reappeared. No one but I seemed to miss him. There was no void left in the carriage, no space where he might have stood. He might just as well have never existed. But that is what the man had done – he had erased his pattern.

You, however, were as beautiful as ever. As summer approached and you shed your heavy coats for lighter wear, I was able to see you shine once more. You were even more important to me now, my sole Subway friend.

And then, one morning, as you were taking your seat, a man pushed past you and set off further down the carriage. You thought nothing of him, I'm sure, beyond a momentary annoyance at his rudeness, but I recognised him. I still could not see his face clearly, but it was evidently the same man. The man who had followed my musical boy. I watched as he continued down the carriage until he was lost in the morning crowd jostling for standing space, and I wondered as to his motives in that action.

    I soon found out. Two days later, I saw him again.

    I was on the same side of the train as you, watching you through the reflection that was cast upon the windows opposite, the dark of the tunnels providing the perfect mirror for the well-lit interior of the train. I knew that here I could see you clearly. And so I could, but also, just to one side of you, I could see a grey figure, apparently just as intent on viewing you. I stared, incredulous, but could not turn to face him without giving myself away. Then suddenly we were out of the tunnel and the returning light of a new station momentarily blinded me. I screwed up my eyes, opening them to a red starburst, but as my vision cleared I saw the man turn away from watching you and shake his head. You were unaware of any of this, and I was powerless to act.

    As time progressed, so I saw the man more often. I do not know if he was aware of me, but he certainly took every opportunity to hide himself. To this day, I still do not know what his face looks like. Yet it was obvious that he was interested in you. And then, one day, a thought occurred to me. If he was watching you here, was he watching you anywhere else? Had he followed you home yet? Did *he* know where you worked?

I could not take that chance. I needed to contact you and warn you of the danger that you are in. So, I wrote you this letter.

By now, you will have probably found my other gift to you as well. I do not know when this man will strike, but I fear for you if he does. There is something about him, a way he has of vanishing, that almost revels in his greyness. It makes him invincible.

But not if you know of him first. Invisibility is his power, so by telling you this I hope to take it away from him. That is why I have also left the knife in your bag. It is there for you to protect yourself, if necessary. I will be here too, but I have no idea if the stranger will attack me as well. He may be too much for me; we may be too evenly matched.

Rest assured, though: I will be watching out for you. I have not slept for some time through worrying about you, but I am determined to be your guardian. Even though I am tired and the threat is close by, I will not waver.

I even have a music machine to listen to, to help to keep me awake. I don't know where it came from and I don't like the music it plays, but it reminds me of the young man and so strengthens my resolve.

He is coming for you. I just want you to know that I am here.

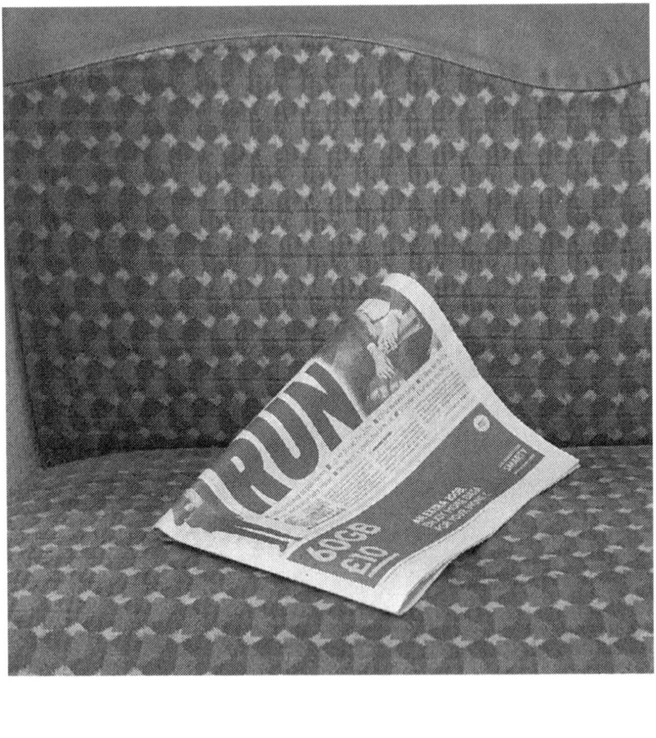
RUN

Buchanan Street to **Hillhead**

"Wonder if the Hag will be there tonight?" Scott says. Adrian smiles at his friend.

"That lanky girl with the bad dress sense?" Davey replies.

Scott shakes his head. "No, *the* Hag," he says, patiently spelling it out. "H.A.G. Hot Asian Guy"

Davey wrinkles his nose. "You're welcome to him. I've heard he swings both ways anyway."

"As long as he swings my way tonight," Scott winks. "I suppose you'll be on the lookout for Smokey?"

Davey flushes slightly. "Nothing wrong with looking."

Adrian smiles at the banter. It is a warm June night and he is wearing his good jeans and a t-shirt with a Keith Haring design on it. Davey wears a Polo shirt and Scott is the only one of them to be wearing a jacket, even if it is Boss.

They are crossing George Square after leaving the Subway. Just three guys out for a night on the town. Except tonight is different, for him at least.

"Which one is Smokey?" he asks.

"He's a bear," Scott jumps in before Davey can answer. "Plus he smells of cigars. *Very* butch. So, Smokey."

"Don't think I've seen him," Adrian says. His friends exchange glances.

"He's only been coming to Del's for the last few weeks," Davey says. "He wasn't there when you were… before."

"Okay," Adrian says. He can see that his friends are feeling awkward, so he moves on quickly. "Well, perhaps I'll put in a good word for you."

"What makes you think he'll be talking to you?" Davey says. "I wouldn't have thought he was your type."

"I'll be fresh meat tonight, guys," Adrian replies. "You know gay memories can't cope with you being off the scene for more than 6 months. Everyone will want to know who I am!"

They laugh and cross the road onto Queen Street. Adrian looks down the road to where it turns onto Ingram Street and his heart stutters slightly in his chest. He makes a fist of one hand, unseen by the others, and presses on.

It had been colder then, the dog days after New Year when no one had any money and everyone needed a party to stave off the January Blues. The ground had glittered with a light frost as Adrian turned into Ingram Street. Like a fairy pathway, he thought and pulled his Puffa jacket around himself to stave off the cold.

That night, he'd been on his own. The plan was to meet Scott at Delmonica's later in the evening (unless either of them got lucky) and then go on to the Polo Lounge, using the passes Del's gave out. It was a tried and trusted formula. No doubt along the way they would pick up other friends too, old and new.

Across the road from Adrian, the high-end clothing shops were all displaying Sale signs which would have been very enticing if they'd been open. Some of the windows still sported Christmas decorations. Even though it was cold, Adrian was glad to be out. A lot of his Christmas had been spent with family and the nagging sense of disappointment he felt from them when his brother and sister both turned up with children in tow. Tonight was for him alone, reconnecting with his world.

He walked along the front of the Mercure Hotel and decided to cut down the side of it to get to the club.

They are turning into Ingram Street now. Scott glances over to Adrian but doesn't say anything.

"Ooh, a sale!" Davey says, pointing across the road to the Boss shop.

"Already looked," Scott says. "Not a lot in it."

"Maybe not in your size," Davey replies and winks at Adrian. Scott punches him on the arm, playfully.

"Bitch," he says.

"On a good day," Davey replies.

Adrian is aware that they are talking to fill the silence, to take his mind off what is to come, and silently he thanks them for that.

They are walking along the front of the Mercure Hotel .

The alley at the side of the hotel had been dark. Strings of small lights had been hung across it – whether they were neglected Christmas decorations or permanent fixtures, Adrian couldn't say – but they didn't really provide much illumination.

There was a fire door for the hotel on his right and another for the Corinthian Club on the left. He could hear the air conditioner above the club door whirring in the night, small puffs of warm air just visible in front of it. Further down the alley, on the left, there were three rubbish skips, one overloaded and spilling out onto the floor.

These were all things that he noticed after, when they were more important. At the time, though, it had just been an alley, Virginia Place Leading To Virginia Street as the sign on the corner told him. He'd cut down it hundreds of times, never given it a thought.

Dimly, just beyond the rubbish bins, Adrian saw the orange glow of a cigarette suddenly blossom into life.

The three of them are standing at the top of Virginia Place.

It is a light night, summer sun pushing their shadows into the alley, but otherwise it has not changed. The bins are still there, still overflowing. The air conditioner still whirrs. It's just an alley, nothing more. And yet.

"Are you okay?" Scott says. Adrian doesn't answer straight away, then he nods.

"You two get on," he says.

They glance at one another. "If you want us..." Scott begins.

Adrian puts a hand on his friend's arm, silencing him, reassuring him. "No, you go the other way. I'll see you at Del's."

Another glance and then Davey breaks from the group, starting off down the street. He stops after a few steps and waits for Scott.

Scott looks at Adrian. They have been friends for years and he wants to stay with him, but he also knows this is something Adrian has to do alone. Reluctantly, he joins Davey and the two of them walk off up the street.

Adrian had been halfway down the alley before he realised there were two men stood by the skips.

It gave him a moment's pause, but nothing more. They were probably smokers who had come out of the hotel for a quick cigarette, or kitchen workers from the club, or even homeless guys. They were not a cause for concern.

As he drew level with them, one of the men flicked a cigarette stub in his path and said, "What've we got here?"

Adrian ignored him and continued walking, but the man stepped out in front of him. Later, when he finally told people about this evening, Adrian found that he couldn't describe the man at all. He was taller than him, that he knew, and he was wearing boots, probably Doc Martins or work boots, but everything else was a blank. Hair colour, hair style, build, clothes – none of them stayed in his mind. It was there on the edges of his memory but for some reason he couldn't see it at all.

"I'm just passing through," Adrian said, adding for no reason "Going to the club."

The man refused to let him pass and Adrian was now aware that the second man had moved around behind him.

"Night out," the first man said. "Must be nice to have the money."

Adrian tried to move around the man but suddenly he felt a hand on his shoulder. The man behind him, restraining him.

Adrian could have shrugged the hand off, tried to make a break for it, pushed past the first guy and bolted to the end of the alley, but he didn't. Later it would haunt him that he just stayed there, passive, sure this was all a joke. He was in a city, near a club, by a main street – it was absurd to think anything could happen to him here.

The first man punched him hard in the stomach. Adrian doubled over, feeling sick as the pain radiated through his body. He looked up in shock.

"Give us your wallet. Now," the man said.

Adrian just stood there, dumbfounded. The first man slapped him hard across the face with the back of his hand. Adrian tasted blood.

"Now!" the man repeated.

Adrian moved a hand to get into his coat where his wallet was, but he was shaking too much to find the zipper.

"Oh, for fuck's sake!" the man said. He brushed Adrian's hand aside and barked "Hold him" at the other man.

Adrian felt strong hands pulling his arms back and then the first man was taking hold of the zip on his coat and roughly pulling it down. Somehow, this was more of an invasion than the punch and Adrian struggled against the grip. The man pulled open his coat and cold air rushed in. The man found the pocket inside the coat and pulled Adrian's wallet out. He opened it.

"No cash," he said. But he pulled Adrian's three credit cards out and stuffed them into his own pocket. Then he pushed his hands inside the coat again, patting Adrian's body down. Adrian shivered as the rough handling continued, the man even putting his hands inside his jeans pockets and pulling the lining out. A few coins clattered to the floor, the noise suddenly louder than it had any right to be.

"Pick it up!" the man snarled. Adrian stared at him and before he knew what was happening the other man was pushing down on his shoulders, forcing him to kneel down on the cracked tarmac. The frosted surface glittered like a thousand tiny knives.

Numbly, Adrian started to pick up the coins and that was when the first kick came. The boot hit him in the side and he immediately curled into a ball. More kicks came, to his back and his chest, to his hands and his face. Both men were kicking him. Distantly he could hear laughter. One of the men stomped down hard on his thigh and he felt his knee twist between the blow and the hard floor. Then one of the boots hit him in the face – he could see it coming in slow motion – and everything went black.

Adrian stands at the edge of the alley and takes a deep breath.

He knows there is no one else there. He knows his attackers are long gone. Logic tells him that this time he is not alone, that his friends will be waiting for him at the other end and that if anything does happen, they will be there to raise the alarm.

He knows all this, but still his feet do not move.

He must only have been out for a few seconds, because when sound and light returned to him, Adrian could see the two men running away. He didn't care. He didn't care about anything beyond the white pain that was pulsing through his body.

Slowly, he uncurled from the foetal position he had pulled himself into. There was liquid on the ground just beside him and for a moment he thought it was raining. Then he realised it was his blood. He reached out carefully to where the man had thrown his wallet down on the tarmac and pulled it in to himself.

It could have been an hour before he sat up, it could have been minutes. Time had lost all meaning.

Eventually, he managed to stand upright, using the bins to pull himself up.

He couldn't put weight on his left leg, so he leant against the skips for a short while until he could figure out how to walk. Somehow, he did. Somehow, he made it back to the Subway station.

Going down the stairs to the platform at Buchanan Street was agony. Each step had to be taken with his right leg first, holding on to the railing for dear life, then bringing his injured leg up to follow. A couple of people passed him on his slow journey down, but no one offered to help.

When he finally got onto the train, Adrian was shocked by the face looking back at him in the window's reflection. One side of his face was starting to puff up and blood and grime was streaked across his cheeks and forehead. Part of his coat was torn, white fluffy filling poking out near his shoulder. But the thing that shocked him the most was the eyes of the man in the reflection. They belonged to a man who was defeated, who had lost everything he had assumed about the world.

It wasn't far to Hillhead but in that journey, Adrian made a decision. He was not going to go to the Police. He was not going to tell anyone about this. He didn't know if the attack had been because he was gay or just because he was in the wrong place at the wrong time, but he wanted it to be over. He didn't want to relive the terror, the shame of it all over again, time after time. He didn't want the questions – *Why didn't you fight back? Why didn't you run?* - because the answers were too terrible for him to contemplate at that time.

By the time Adrian got himself home, he wanted nothing more than to curl up in his bed. He didn't expect to sleep, but somehow, as soon as he lay down, fully clothed and unwashed, darkness mercifully took over.

The next few days were a symphony in pain. He rang into work and told them he was feeling ill. They weren't happy but they had no choice in the matter. There was no way he could go in, not looking like he did. He couldn't even take a Zoom call. Three days in, however, and even Adrian recognised he had to get medical help. His leg was no better and he was having trouble breathing sometimes. He sat for an hour after he made the decision, listening to his laboured breathing but not wanting to leave his room, before he called a taxi and went to A&E.

He recognised the nurse who saw him from the apps. Probably Growlr given his chunky build. At any other time, Adrian would have flirted with him, but his thoughts were elsewhere. The nurse was kind and asked how the injuries had happened. Adrian refused to say but he knew the man had guessed the cause even before asking.

Doctors were called, but the nurse stayed with him all day, occasionally dealing with other patients but always calling back to check on him. He quietly but persistently lobbied for Adrian to contact the Police, but he refused. Finally, six hours after arriving, Adrian left with a splint on his leg and wealth of painkillers and antiseptics.

He went back to his flat and stayed there for two months.

He wants his legs to move. He wants this to be over with, to close this chapter, to start to move beyond it. Still, he stands at the threshold of the alley.

Adrian remembers the months that followed the attack. The slow process of healing physically; the friends who helped him to heal in other ways. Scott and Davey had been appalled when they heard, but never once did they tell him to report the incident, never once did they push him to do more than he wanted to. They had been by his side, patient and full of good humour, for the six months since the attack, and he knew he could never thank them enough.

Although he had eventually left his flat, this was the first time he had been back into town. The Christmas decorations were gone, but rainbow flags had taken their place. When you're gay, there's a lot of talk about Pride, with a capital P, and rightly so. But sometimes the word overshadowed the meaning. Pride was about the fight as much as the celebration. Pride was about being confident in yourself, whether that meant your sexuality or just being able to walk safely down a street. Pride was about knowing yourself. Pride was what they had taken from him.

Adrian takes a step forward. He feels as if he has pushed through some invisible barrier. He can still feel its pull on him, calling him back to the shame and the solitude, but as he takes another step, it weakens.

He is level with the hotel Fire Door now. Adrian is aware that his heart is beating fast. His skin feels sweatier than the mild June night calls for. But he can't turn back.

He is next to the first rubbish skip. The lid is closed and for a moment he feels like stopping and leaning on it, gathering his breath. Instead, he presses on. The third skip is open and paper and food waste spills out over the top of it. A brief summer breeze catches the smell and pushes it towards Adrian. It is sweet and rotten at the same time and, in the moment he smells it, he is transported back to that night, to pulling himself upright on the bin and smelling that same odour. Terror falls on him, making him briefly feel sick. He looks up, almost expecting to see a boot coming towards his face, searching for someone hiding on the other side of the bins.

There is nothing. The alley is quiet and empty. Another breeze sends the smell away and Adrian breathes deeply of the cool night air. He presses on.

As he reaches the end of the alley, it feels like he has run a marathon. He looks back at the path he has taken. It looks so ordinary now, so mundane.

Just around the corner, not wishing to surprise him, Scott and Davey are waiting.

They look at him with relief and love.

"So," Scott says. "Ready to get your dancing shoes on?"

Adrian looks at him and smiles. For the first time in a long time, that is exactly what he feels like doing.

PASSENGERS ARE WARNED TO STAND CLEAR OF THE GATES.

Copland Road to **Partick Cross**

"But will there be elephants?"

George's Mum nodded to him as she paid her 20p to get on the Subway. The lady in the ticket office hardly glanced at her as the machine clattered and spat out her ticket.

"And lions and tigers," Grandad said, as he fumbled in his pocket.

"Oh, for goodness sake," Mum said. "You could have got your money ready."

Grandad pulled some change out. "I'm still not used to this new money," he said and put a bunch of mixed coins, old and new money, down on the counter. He winked at his grandson as he did so and George suspected that Grandad actually knew all about decimalisation, he was just being awkward because he didn't like it. The Ticket lady glanced at Mum but still sorted through the change for the correct amount, pushing the rest back towards Grandad.

"Come on," Mum said. "The train'll be here in a minute."

She had a firm hand on George's shoulder to stop him running off ahead of them. The eight-year-old knew better but still could hardly contain his excitement. He was supposed to have gone to the Circus at Kelvin Hall the previous year, but he'd been ill with the flu at the time and had to sit it out (no amount of protestations had helped him - his Mum had used the unbeatable logic of 'If you're well enough to go to the Circus, you're well enough to go to School' and George had crumbled). Having waited a whole year for the opportunity to come around again, he was now desperate to get on the Subway.

As Grandad now had his ticket, the three of them descended the stairs to the platform. Going on the Subway was a treat in itself for George, who otherwise walked everywhere. To him, the peeling paint on the walls was unimportant, the grey colour of the station with its pale blue tiles was merely background. The station was a strange, magical, subterranean world, light streaming into it through skylights cut into the ceiling, the central platform dappled with the reflections of the rain on their glass. The air smelt musty and, even though there were only a few people on the platform, George could feel the presence of the hundreds of people who used the Subway every day.

There was a deep rumble from the tunnel and, with a screech of brakes, the train arrived. Its bright red livery shone under the sunlight, bringing a shot of colour to the drabness. Each carriage had two doors, one at either end, and Grandad rushed over to the nearest, pulling back the iron grating and ushering Mum and George in.

George loved going into the carriage – the white curved ceiling, the dark wood panelling, the deep red leather seats all made it feel like he was entering the world of the Grown Ups, a special place that he was being given temporary access to. It didn't matter that the leather was cracked and old, or that the place smelt faintly of sweat, cigarettes and oil – these were all things that he wouldn't normally experience. He glanced at his fellow passengers and saw that none of them were excited by the ride, the magical made commonplace in their eyes.

His Mum pushed him down into a seat and sat herself next to him. Grandad sat opposite them, underneath a sign proclaiming No Spitting. The train pulled away.

The journey was only four stops – Copland Road, Govan Cross, Merkland Street and, finally, Partick Cross. It didn't take long but George drank in every second of it. He noticed the woman sat just beyond Grandad who kept nervously touching her scarf, the hair underneath it shaped into rigid curls, lacquered to within an inch of its life. George saw the young man at the far end of the carriage, with his fashionable denims flared out before him, the hems almost sweeping the dust off the floor when he stood up to leave. George admired the man's long hair, spilling over his collar, and wished that his Mum would let him have hair like that. He'd argued once that it would save them money because he wouldn't have to go to the barbers for a short back and sides as often, but the plea fell on deaf ears. Instead, he continued to suffer the barber pushing his head down with one hand, heavy rings pressing into his skull, whilst he shaved him from nape to crown.

All too soon, the trip was over and the family emerged into the curious little alley that housed Partick Cross station. From the outside, the only sign that the Subway was there was a large circular street sign with a prominent red U. As they emerged onto Dumbarton Road, between two shops, household goods to the left, clothes to the right, a large drop of water hit George on the forehead.

"Better get a move on," Grandad said, "It's dreich."

Mum tugged at the front of her scarf as if that would have made the flimsy nylon cloth somehow rainproof and led the way out into the street.

By the time they got to the front of Kelvin Hall, the rain was coming down harder. For George, however, the darkened skies only served to highlight the wonder of the Halls. The streets outside and the front of the building were festooned with coloured lights, twinkling against the darkening skies. Some went on and off in sequence, creating the image of a fan unfolding or a rainbow growing from purple up to red, whereas others were pictures – of clowns, lions, horses – backlit and reflected in the damp pavements.

"Gets more like ruddy Blackpool every year," Grandad said as they ducked under the great-columned entrance, where taxis usually idled for those that could afford them.

George only had eyes for one illumination, though. To the left of the lion, right next to the word *Circus* which overshadowed all the other signs, was an elephant. All his life, George had been entranced by elephants. He had been given a small soft toy elephant when he was a baby, so long ago that it had always been part of his world, and this had become the start of a fascination. The grey corduroy of the toy had worn smooth in places, one ear hanging awry after a neighbour's dog had gotten hold of it, but it was still a precious thing to George. He watched *Animal Magic* on the television every week with Johnny Morris talking to and with the animals of Bristol Zoo, just in case he should chat with an elephant. When he did, and the elephant spoke with sonorous and slow words, only slightly betrayed by a Welsh accent, George felt a chill run up his spine.

"Come on," said Mum. "I don't want to hang around out here, getting cold" and she pulled George into the waves of people streaming into the building, all – like him – eager to follow the lights into a fantasy wonderland.

The first thing to hit George was the chaos of the interior. The three of them had walked into a huge fairground housed within the building. The noise of people and machines, the sound of music competing with songs from other rides, the clang of bells and shriek of whistles was overwhelming. George could see some dodgem cars, and two carousels – one with the traditional horses and one with a variety of animals to ride on – and innumerable stalls pushing everything from candyfloss to ball games. Right next to him was a shooting gallery, eager young boys queuing up to try and hit playing card targets, desperate to win one of the goldfish that hung in water-filled plastic bags from the stall's frame.

"Do you want a go?" Grandad asked.

George looked up at him excitedly, but Mum stepped in. "He's not old enough to be shooting guns," she said. "Let's see what else there is."

Grandad looked like he wanted to argue the point but thought better of it. Mum took him over to one of the carousels.

"Here, this looks nice," she said as the cavalcade of animals came to a halt beside her. "Look, they've even got an elephant!"

George perked up at the word. Honestly, he thought he was too old for the ride, but he looked over and there was indeed an elephant on it. It was more blue than grey in colour with large heavily-lashed eyes. Its trunk was raised so that it was parallel to the pole that fastened it to the top of the ride, and it had tiny white tusks. George went straight over to it, ignoring his Grandad shaking his head, and climbed on to the elephant's hard plastic back whilst his Mum paid the man working the ride. It wasn't particularly comfortable and some of the paint had been worn off the seat revealing the white plastic underneath what was supposed to be a saddle, but George loved it. As the ride started up and the elephant started to move up and down, he imagined that this would be what it was like to ride the real thing.

When the ride stopped, it was evident that Mum and Grandad had 'had words'. This was something that happened quite often these days, usually out of sight of George, and usually about him. This time it seemed that Grandad had prevailed, because their next visits were to the less-stately pleasures of the dodgems and a Wurlitzer. George enjoyed both of them, although the Wurlitzer did make him feel slightly queasy. Grandad joined him on both, his face a broad grin as he bashed into him as often as possible on the dodgems, but Mum stayed outside the rides, her face set into a neutral glower.

When the two of them came down off a Caterpillar ride that used a canopy to cover the riders halfway through, forcing George to experience the undulations of the track in delicious darkness, Mum said, "We need to be going. It's almost time."

For a moment, George thought they were about to leave, but then he realised what she meant: it was almost time for the circus. An illuminated sign proclaiming *Kelvin Hall Circus 1971!* had teased him throughout all his time on the rides, so he knew the entrance to the Circus was over at the back of the

Fairground Hall, just to the left. There were two performance times a day and they were set to visit the evening show.

The three of them joined a queue to get into the arena and Mum bought a programme from a girl stood by the door as they entered. It cost 3d – a sum that seemed to please Grandad, presumably because it was still in money that he approved of.

The Arena was the biggest room that George had ever been in. As they took their place at the back of the raised bank of seating, he marvelled at the circular ring in the centre of the room, its thick low walls surrounding a space filled with sand and sawdust. He noticed the boxes behind and above him, where he assumed impossibly wealthy people would watch the show, and the band of musicians over in one corner of the room, grandly billed as The Circus Orchestra, dwarfed by the space they were playing in.

The show began with a Ringmaster welcoming the audience. He was a tall, slim man who wore a top hat and a red tailcoat with blue lapels. George thought he might be the most sophisticated man he'd ever seen. The Ringmaster's round vowels and expansive hand gestures, accented by his white gloves, filled the arena so that all eyes were upon him.

The first act he introduced was an acrobatic duo with the exotic-sounding names of Domenico and Juanita. The two of them pirouetted around the ring, balancing on cylinders and see-saws, Domenico frequently hoisting his partner onto his shoulders from which she would leap to some new precarious position. The crowd 'oohed' at every leap and broke into applause frequently.

After a little while, George realised that a lot of the Circus involved acrobats – on the trapeze or a high wire, juggling clubs or rolling around the ring on giant balls – but, good as they were, he knew they were not what the audience were there for. Similarly, the clowns who jumped out every now and then with slapstick vignettes, designed to entertain the audience while the red-shirted Ring Boys removed or placed the props for the next act, were funny but also slightly scary. It wasn't just that George felt they could come into the audience at any point, trailing anarchy with them, it was their make-up – a face stencilled over a face, a grin fixed over anger or sadness – that worried him.

No, the audience were waiting for the animals.

Things started small. Early on in the show, a woman called Phyllis Allan brought out her trained Poodles, a pack of clipped and coiffured dogs of varying sizes who did balancing tricks or caught flaming torches, all for the reward of a piece of cheese. George had a dog back at home, a mongrel called Blackie, and he couldn't imagine his dog walking from one side of the room to the other on command, so he thought Phyllis Allan's Poodles were amazing.

After these came the horses, prancing around the ring and moving in smooth synchronicity, to the commands of Enrico Caroli and his family. This display of majesty and grace was immediately followed by a troupe of Welsh Ponies, stubby little clown horses that the audience took to immediately.

All of this was fine and entertaining, but George was still waiting for the main act. He'd seen dogs and horses before, could see them every day if he wanted to – what he wanted was an elephant.

Very soon, he got his wish. The Ringmaster stepped back into the ring, shooing a couple of tumbling clowns away first, and announced: "Ladies and Gentlemen! Prepare to be astounded by our next act – a display of Pachydermian prowess and mammoth majesty rarely seen in this country! Glasgow, I give you – Sir Robert Fossett's Elephants!"

George felt his breath catch in his throat as the spotlights swung away from the Ringmaster and over to the entrance from behind the Circus. The band struck up a version of *The Baby Elephant Walk* (which George recognised from a film he had seen on tv) and then, suddenly, there they were.

George wasn't prepared for the size of the animals. He'd known they were big, of course, but somehow that had not translated to the beast before him. The elephants – six in total – came out one by one, moving slowly into the ring. George was struck by how graceful they were, how gentle their footsteps seemed despite the weight being put on them. Their skin looked tough, and yet sagged and gathered at the joints like silk. Everything about them was both familiar and new. George was entranced.

The elephants waited patiently as someone George assumed was Sir Robert Fossett, a man dressed in the sort of African gamekeeper's outfit he had seen on *Daktari*, arranged them into a row curling around the ring. He introduced each of them – Dum Dum, Sara, Emma, Bindula, Mahala and Minnie – and at the sound of their name each beast dropped to one knee, all standing up again as one at his final command.

Then came the tricks. One elephant, Dum Dum, stood on her hind legs and gently, slowly spun around, her trunk high in the air. Two others pushed a ball between each other before one flicked it forcefully with her trunk into a set of goal nets brought in by the Ring Boys. After a few more tricks, including Bindula spraying the audience with water from her trunk and causing a lot of screaming and giggles, it came to the finale of the act.

Two platforms were set up with parallel ropes running taut between them, and two small pedestals placed beside each platform. The main platforms were also secured to the ground with thick ropes and hooks. Minnie was brought forward. Like Bindula and Mahala, she was an Indian elephant, immediately recognisable to George for her smaller ears. She dutifully stepped up onto the first platform and then used that to get onto the main one. The trainer stepped forward and held out a long baton with a ball at each end. Minnie took it and, to the delight of the audience, started to twirl it around with her trunk. After a moment she steadied it and, with a command from the trainer, started to walk the double tightrope before her.

It wasn't a long walk, nor was it very high off the ground, but George was thrilled by it. He watched as the great animal used the baton to steady herself, moving slowly and gracefully over the ropes. Her massive feet were still a lot wider than even the thick cords and he could see that it was not easy for her. When she finally reached the second pedestal, George realised that he had been holding his breath the whole time.

With the elephants gone, the rest of the show went by in a blur. George vaguely remembered a woman with some trained doves, more antics from the clowns, some trick cyclists and a troupe of sea lions who barked like dogs and threw a ball around. All of it paled into the background by comparison.

As they were getting up to leave, the band still playing and the sound of applause ringing in their ears, Grandad said, "Well, it was alright but there were no lions this year."

George hadn't even thought about that. "But the elephants were amazing," he said.

"Do you want to go and see one?" Grandad said, and Mum shot him a look.

"It's getting late," she said, "And he's excited enough. He'll never get to sleep at this rate."

"It'll only be a few minutes, doll," Grandad replied. "It might not even be there."

Mum scowled. "Well, I'm not going. The smell was bad enough in here."

Grandad winked at George. "This way, boy," he said and the two of them went off on their own.

They stepped through a door in a much larger wrought iron gate into what looked like a yard or a car park at the back of Kelvin Halls. The rain was still coming down, running in rivulets between the cobblestones. It was lighter than before, but George could tell Grandad probably didn't want to stay out in it for too long even so. The yard wasn't particularly large, but it led out on one side to another area where George could just see a series of cages and trucks. He could hear the barking of the sea lions mingling with the yapping of what he assumed were the poodles of earlier. Some horse boxes were visible, pushed into a corner, and beside them there were a couple of huge trucks, their roofs peeking over the dividing wall.

The main attraction, however, was over in the opposite corner. An elephant stood on its own in a small enclosure that had been created between the outside walls and a chain strung between posts. A sign hung on the chain said 'Do Not Feed The Animals'. If it had wanted to, the elephant could have easily pushed through the chain and gone anywhere, but instead it just stood there, in the rain, tail swishing slowly, its trunk picking at the dusty ground.

There was a small crowd by the chain already. As they joined them, George heard a noise from one of the trucks over by the other wall and realised that the other elephants were probably in there. Just beside it, there was a pile of what looked like large brown balls and a sign saying 'Elephant dung – good for the garden. Help yourself!'

Being small, he was able to push his way to the front of the crowd, whilst Grandad had to follow slightly behind.

Up close, George could see the elephant in more detail. A slight whitening on the tips of her ears identified her as Minnie, the tightrope walker. Perhaps it was the rain or the fact that her trainer wasn't present, but Minnie looked sad. He could see her brown eyes, looking down and ignoring the people pointing and talking about her in the rain. Just as the clowns' eyes had scared him for showing what lived under their mask, so seeing Minnie's eyes spoke to something inside him by showing an intelligence behind hers.

A man stood next to George said, "Doesn't do much, does it?"

George wasn't sure if the man was talking to him, but he decided not to reply. The man didn't seem to expect an answer anyway. He took a long drag on his cigarette and then flicked the lit stub towards Minnie. It landed, still smoking, just by her front leg.

For a moment, it seemed as if the elephant hadn't noticed, but then her trunk moved up and away from the offending smell. Minnie brought one leg up slightly and looked as if she was going to stomp on the cigarette butt, yet instead she let her foot hover over it for a second. With a shake of her head, she pulled her foot away and moved her position so as to be further away from the lit remains.

With a shock, George realised that she had not stood on the butt because she had felt the heat coming from it on the soles of her feet. He had assumed that her large flat feet were hard and insensitive from carrying so much weight, but here Minnie was demonstrating that she could even feel something as small as that. And with this realisation came another. If her feet were that sensitive, how painful must it be for her to walk on those narrow ropes night after night, sometimes twice a day?

George looked over at Minnie and for the first time saw not a pet, not a toy, not a funny talking zoo animal, but a living being, with feelings and intelligence and a life all her own. A life she probably shouldn't be living, not in Glasgow or at any Circus. George couldn't put words to it then, but later in life he remembered the elephant as having a nobility to her, a self-awareness that he had never even guessed at until that day.

He felt a hand on his shoulder and looked back to see his Grandad. The smoker also looked round and then pushed his way past to leave the crowd. George was happy to see him go.

"We should get back to your Mum," Grandad said.

George nodded and took one more look at Minnie. The rain had put the cigarette out now but small tendrils of noxious smoke still rose from it and the elephant was still eyeing it cautiously. So small a thing to have such an effect on so large an animal.

Before today, George probably would have waved goodbye as he left, but now it seemed wrong. Something a kid would do because they thought the elephant was some jolly beast who was just there to entertain them.

Instead, he turned away with his Grandad and headed back to a Subway that felt just a little less magical now.

Authors' Note:

In case you are looking at the modern Subway map and wondering why you can't see the stations mentioned in this story, they are still there but the names have changed. In the late 1970s, with the arrival of the main Partick station as a transport hub and the modernisation of the Subway system, Copland Road became Ibrox, Govan Cross was extensively rebuilt and shortened to just Govan, Merkland Street closed and became Partick, and Partick Cross turned into Kelvinhall.

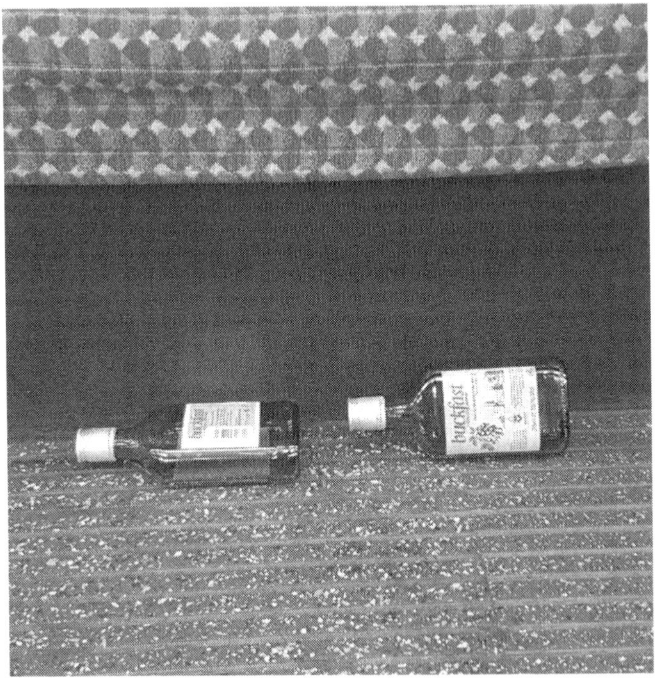
buckfast

Partick to Partick

Mama Used To Say – Junior (1982)

"It's ma Maw. Ma Maw."

Jonno eyed up the man who was talking to him. Just beyond him, Figgsy was nudging the blue-haired guy in the ribs and laughing at the situation.

"Sorry?" Jonno said, and immediately cursed under his breath. First rule of meeting a Subway Loony: Don't Engage.

The man was thin and wiry. He had grey hair with a floppy, slightly greasy fringe, and two-day old stubble on his chin. He was wearing jeans and a t-shirt saying 'No Fear' and his eyes seemed to be constantly searching the length of the rail carriage.

In contrast, Jonno was dressed in a neon pink t-shirt, bright yellow short shorts, leg warmers and a mullet wig which he had tinted with red streaks. Perfect for the 80's themed Sub Crawl that he was on but not the attire of someone a stranger would normally seek out to start a conversation with.

"I hed tae phone the hospital, the hospital", the man was saying. "Ma Maw is in there with the Covid. She's dying with the Covid. I wuz gunny phone, but they phoned me."

Figgsy was killing himself with laughter behind the man and trying to get the rest of the group to listen in, but the noise of the carriage and their mobile DJ meant that he ended up relaying the words back to everyone. Jonno gave him a sharp glance and shook his head to tell him to stop.

Unfortunately, the man misinterpreted his actions.

"No pal, no. Don't be like tha'. I dinna want anythin'. I'm just telling you about ma Maw."

"I wasn't," Jonno began, but stopped. He was only going one stop, he could hear the man out. "Go on," he said.

"So the hospital, they phoned me. An' I thought, this is it the noo. Ma Maw was deed from the Covid. But it wasnee. They were tellin' me she wuz alright. She was comin' haim."

The man smiled at Jonno and his eyes briefly ceased their search of the carriage. He looked straight at Jonno and there was real relief in his eyes. Jonno was surprised to find himself feeling absurdly happy for the man.

"But ye don't wanna be havin' those jags, pal."

The man put a hand on Jonno's arm to impress the seriousness of his words.

"Ma Maw, she had both the jags, the two at the start. Then another two. She had six, 'cos they gave her another two affer tha'. Six jags and she still got the Covid. So don't you be havin' those jags, pal."

Jonno was a biology student and his heart sank a little at the turn the conversation had taken. He was half tempted to try and argue the case for immunisation when he realised that the train was pulling into a station.

"Is tha' Heeheed?" the man said.

Jonno nodded.

"I gotta go to Heeheed," the man continued. "Ma Maw lives there."

The man put his hand out and, automatically, Jonno shook it. It was strangely clammy and the touch made his stomach flop a bit. Instantly, he regretted it. The train shuddered to a stop.

"Nae jags. Remember, pal," the man repeated and then he was off the train and onto the platform.

Jonno looked over at Figgsy. His frend was grinning wildly.

"Come on," he said. "Let's see what 'Heeheed' has to offer."

It's My Life – Talk Talk (1984)

Hillhead was the group's third stop on their Sub Crawl. Fifteen students ("One for each station!" Figgsy had claimed), all dressed with an 80s theme, even though none of them were old enough to have known the era. As a result, some of the sartorial choices were definitely more 70s in nature (Obbo's flared trousers were a real give away, although he claimed he was "on the cusp") and some even touched the 90s (Kelly's tube top was generally acknowledged to be inconsistent with the theme - but the boys were extremely willing to let it pass all the same). No one really cared – a Sub Crawl was just an excuse to raid a few charity shops, dress up and get completely rat-arsed.

The organiser for the evening, as with most group activities, was Figgsy. He had been the one to ring ahead to some of the pubs to make sure that they would get in, no matter how late in the journey they arrived or how worse for wear they were. He had also been the one to suggest the 80s theme and to insist that they bring their own DJ to soundtrack the night. To that end, a friend of his was armed with a powerful wireless speaker and a classic playlist to blast everyone in the carriage with 'mood music', whether their fellow passengers wanted it or not.

It was Figgsy too who had decided the menu for the night: shots in the first pub, beer in the next three, wine in the next three, whisky in the next four ('one extra in a tribute to Scotland'), and cocktails in the next three before finishing with shots again in the final pub.

Like his friend, Jonno had also planned for the evening. He was determined to make it round all 15 stations, with the obligatory stop in a pub at each, and still remember it the day after. To this end, he had started the night by eating three large pots of unsweetened Greek yogurt to get a good balance of protein, fat and carbs into his system. He was not a great drinker but he knew that protein was especially slow to digest and could therefore stave off the effects of alcohol, so he also downed a strawberry protein shake to round things off. He had started the evening feeling full but confident.

It didn't last long. Jonno wasn't sure if some of the yogurt had been off or if the combination of beer and tequila shots was reacting badly with it but, whatever the reason, his stomach was feeling a little queasy.

By the time they all raucously returned to the station after drinking in Jinty McGuinty's Irish Bar, the feeling had increased.

I Want A Dog – Pet Shop Boys (1987)

The train to Kelvinbridge was quieter than the previous one and most of the group took the chance to sit down.

Jonno didn't really trust his stomach with sudden moves so he elected to stay by the doors with Figgsy.

"Okay, nerd - Favourite Power Rangers series?" Figgsy said.

The two had known each other for two terms now and were planning on moving into new accommodation together for the next year. They had an easy-going friendship that looked like it would grow over many years.

"Wild Force," Jonno answered without hesitation. "I used to fancy White Tiger Wild something rotten."

Figgsy laughed. "Not my type," he said. "Not my series. SPD all the way."

"Wasn't that the one with the dog?" Jonno said.

Figgsy laughed. "Anubis 'Doggie' Cruger! Yes. He was cool."

"And I'm the nerd?" Jonno laughed. "I always used to wonder what happened to his nose."

Figgsy looked at him with a raised eyebrow.

"Well, when he suited up, the helmet was flat, but out of it, he had a snout," Jonno explained.

"That's why they call them *Morphing* Power Rangers," Figgsy answered.

"Yeah, but..."

"Don't overthink it," Figgsy smiled and clapped a hand on his friend's shoulder. "Anyway, we're here."

As the train pulled into Kelvinbridge station, Figgsy turned to the rest of the group and shouted "Rise and shine, boys and girls! Last of the beer stops!"

Hungry Like The Wolf – Duran Duran (1982)

By the time the group had left The Laurieston Bar and were heading back to Bridge Steet station, Jonno was not feeling at all well. Somewhere along the way, he had lost his wig and the group had lost two people. Nine stations in, now officially across the river, and on their second whisky venue, it felt as if they had been out for days rather than hours. The fact that it seemed to have gone dark between entering The Laurieston and leaving it only compounded the matter.

Jonno was standing in the car park beside the station when Figgsy walked up.

"Lost another one," he said with a cheery smile. "Obbo's heading home. Lightweight."

Jonno steadied himself on a nearby bollard and nodded.

"Some of the others have just nipped to the falafel place up the road to get some food," Figgsy continued. "Do you want any?"

Jonno thought of the spiced food they would be returning with and his stomach did a flip. He fought back a wave of nausea and shook his head.

"You okay?" said Figgsy. "You look a bit green around the gills."

"No, I'm fine," Jonno replied. "Just coming out into the night air."

Figgsy looked at him for a second, then slapped his friend heartily on the back. Jonno tasted rancid yogurt and struggled to keep it down. He was about to say that he too would head home, but at that point the rest of the group returned. Figgsy greeted them with a cry of "Onwards!" and disappeared inside the Subway entrance.

Taking a deep breath of the cool air, Jonno followed him.

Fashion – David Bowie (1980)

It was on the train from Kinning Park that Jonno realised how much he had managed to drink.

Until that point, he had been more concerned with his stomach, but after the Moscow Mule he had downed in The Bellrock, the focus shifted. The Mule had been sweet, spicy and – above all – strong. Suddenly, the world was just a little less stable.

The man sat opposite Jonno was wearing trousers that mixed a cream floral print with large brown corduroy patches. They tumbled over a pair of good quality boots, whilst above them he was wearing a cable knit jumper under a zip up hoodie and a denim overjacket. It takes a lot of money to look that shambolic, Jonno thought, but sartorial elegance was actually furthest from his mind. He was more concerned with the way the floral pattern on the guy's trousers was crawling across his legs.

Jonno shook his head and looked over to where Figgsy was wrapped around Kelly a little further down the carriage. The act of doing this made the world blur until his gaze settled and everything crowded back into place.

I think I may be drunk, Jonno thought. Perhaps I should tell someone.

But before he could catch this thought and do something about it, the train pulled to a stop.

Self Control – Laura Branigan (1984)

Govan was the last drinking stop of the night. By this point, there were only 6 of the original group left and the power had died on the DJ's speakers, but for Jonno and Figgsy the night had been a success.

The Brechins Bar had been the perfect final stop – a forbidding slab of Glasgow architecture from the outside but warm and welcoming inside. The remaining revellers had downed their Jager Bombs and overenthusiastically congratulated each other on making it all the way round the Subway loop. They were even on time to get back to the Subway before the last train of the night left to return everyone to Partick and their beds.

Jonno could still taste the liquorice of the Jagermeister shot as he stood on the platform and waited for the train to arrive. It was quite agreeable. The buzz from the Red Bull would carry him home and then, with luck, it would wear off enough to let him sleep. All was good with the world.

He looked across to Figgsy who was snogging Kelly over by the wall. Jonno smiled. He thought Figgsy was a great friend and he felt he really should go over and tell him that. Perhaps hug him. Hug Kelly too. In fact, Jonno would be happy to hug everyone on the platform. Alcohol was a wonderful thing.

The train pulled in before him and, as the doors slid open, Jonno stepped forward to get on.

A passenger, tall and solid, ran straight into him as he was getting off.

"Oot tha fuckin' way!" the man said.

Jonno stood for a moment and stared at him. He was taller than Jonno, older by a few years, hair cropped close to his head and a tattoo snaking its way down his neck into his shirt. Jonno was confused. He briefly wondered if he should hug this man too.

"Did ye no hear me?" the man said. "Move!"

The man could have easily stepped around Jonno on the platform, but instead he was insisting that he move. It didn't make sense. Jonno shook his head and moved forward to get into the carriage. He had intended to go round the man, but walking was not his forte by this point and as he passed his shoulder caught the man on the chest.

The man spun round as Jonno stepped onto the train. He grabbed Jonno by the shoulder and turned him so the two were facing one another again. Unfortunately, this was the biggest mistake he could have made.

As Jonno was whirled around, his stomach decided that this was the time to be noticed again. Suddenly the taste of liquorice in his mouth was overwhelmed by a cocktail of wine, whisky, and yogurt. Jonno noted in a disinterested way that there was nothing he could do about what was coming next. He just had to open his mouth.

The torrent of vomit hit the man squarely in the chest. Jonno could feel it emptying from his stomach and with this came a sense of lightness and pleasure.

Bright colours suffused the scene and Jonno had the strange notion that he was allowing something wild and beautiful into the world.

The man had a different point of view. He staggered backwards onto the platform, his shirt drenched, a scrap of undigested tomato skin clinging to his eyebrow, just as the doors slid back together, separating the two of them once more. As the train pulled away, Jonno saw him rush towards the carriage but then they were in the tunnel and the man had gone.

The last thing Jonno remembered was Figgsy rushing towards him as the darkness of the tunnels crept in through the windows and surrounded them.

Wake Me Up Before You Go-Go – Wham! (1984)

Jonno dreamt of being half-carried, half-walked off a Subway train. Figgsy was there, and Kelly, and the DJ guy, and possibly some other people too but they were just shadowy figures at the sides of his dream. Then the dream made a jump-cut to the exterior of his flat and Figgsy was trying to get a key into the door. He seemed to take a long, long time to do it, but then suddenly Jonno was inside and on his bed and the room was spinning around him like a kaleidoscope made up of everything he owned.

Jonno opened his eyes. The room was still now, but the sun was stabbing its way in through the half-open blinds at his window. Groggily, he reached up and pulled the cord that closed them completely. Blissful darkness descended.

His eyes once more closed, Jonno's other senses rushed forward to fill the gap. It smelt like something had died somewhere and, from the taste of it, Jonno wasn't sure that it hadn't happened in his mouth. He worked his jaw for a moment, freeing up the stiffness that seemed to have set in.

A groan came from somewhere to his right. Gingerly, Jonno turned his head to see what had made the sound.

Figgsy was sprawled across the floor by his side. Jonno reached round and pulled a pillow from behind his head, then threw it at his friend. Figgsy made a grumpy snorting noise but otherwise stayed asleep.

Jonno put his head back down and decided to wait it out. It was Sunday, there was no rush. Classes were tomorrow's problems and, for now, he could relax, lie back and think about how he had survived his first Sub Crawl.

His *first* Sub Crawl.

Yes, he was definitely going to do this again…

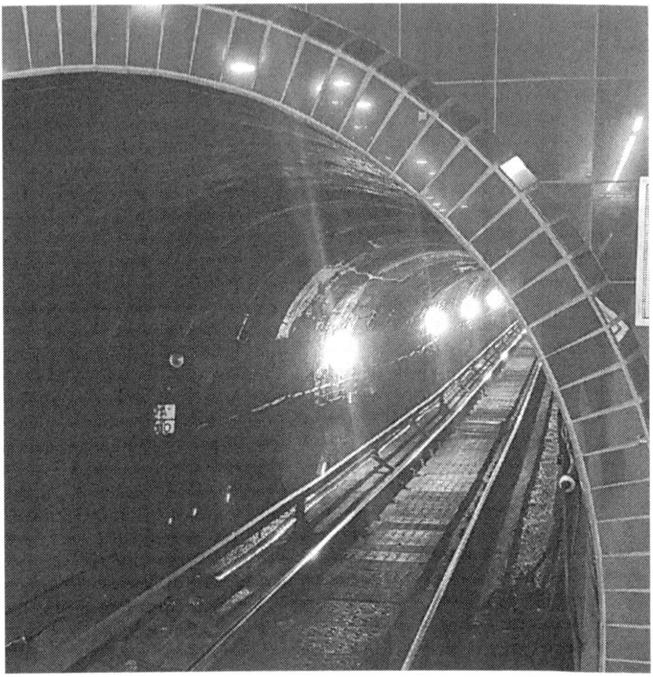

Govan to Partick

I don't know where it started.

It could have been the lecture, it could have been when I met Susan. It could have been even earlier than that.

I know where it ended, though.

With me never setting foot in that damned Subway ever again.

I only went to the lecture because of Susan. At that point we had been going out for four months – long enough to have settled into one another and to have found the rhythms of the relationship, but not to have found any jarring differences. We were still at that stage where we found the other's foibles amusing rather than problematic, so when she said she'd like to go to a talk at a bookshop, I volunteered to tag along without checking what it was.

The talk was at a small Indie bookshop in the Merchant City, one of those that didn't bother with bestsellers but instead sought out limited editions, small print runs, and obscure authors. There was a decent turn out as well – about thirty people, comfortably packed into the main shop space on mismatched chairs. The shop owner was selling cups of tea and instant coffee off to one side of the room.

I confess, when I first arrived, my heart sank. It didn't seem like my kind of audience. There was an abundance of tie-dyed clothing and coloured hair. I don't want to sound like an old fogey, but I'm an Economics student and most of the people I know look like proto-accountants, all just waiting for that magical spreadsheet to enter their lives and bestow the Business Suit of Doom upon them. In that sense, Susan – as an Arts student, a Theatre Major even – was way outside my comfort zone. But still, we worked as a couple and if she wanted to come to a talk frequented by Glasgow's answer to Woodstock, who was I to argue?

The title of the book, displayed in a haphazard pile on a desk beside a microphone, was 'The Psychogeography of Albion – How Britain Became Haunted'. Personally, I would have thought the subtitle would have been better up front, but when I saw the author, I could see why such showmanship was probably beyond him.

Bernard Keir looked like he belonged to my tribe. Think Peter Cushing playing a Scottish solicitor – a grey three piece suit over a spindly figure, wispy hair that had faded to grey long ago, kindly eyes set deep in a face that had been pulled gaunt by age. He looked out of place amongst the riot of colour that had come to see him, like a lecturer at a very progressive school. Five minutes into his talk, however, and I could see how apt this description was. He was deathly boring.

I didn't take in a lot of his talk. There was mention of ley lines and psychogeography, tales of pagan pathways and solstice sacrifices. Most of it washed over me, but Keir seemed to be saying that he thought we all had a collective memory of ancient mythical beings or forces. Whether you called them Elder Gods or collective manifestations of the Unconscious, he believed that primitive man lived in fear of these creatures and devised ways, through ritual and rite, to bind them, to reduce their power. Even though these beings were forgotten now, modern man still went through the motions of controlling them, be it through Solstice festivals or regular gatherings like Fairs, unaware that we were re-enacting ancient spells but upholding the tradition, nonetheless. Ghosts, he said, were just smaller versions of this, glimpsed moments of something greater, localised and held in place by geography or bricks and mortar.

There was a lot of vigorous nodding at parts of his talk, and I could see that, for the main, he was preaching to the converted, even if I thought it was, frankly, bollocks. I couldn't tell if Susan was as convinced but she didn't yawn as much as me so she must have had some interest in what he was talking about.

Finally, the talk ended and, to polite applause, Keir agreed to take questions. There were a few raised hands and, surprisingly, I found mine to be among them.

Susan stared at me – I think she thought I was going to be rude to him – but my hand stayed up even after two other people had been chosen. Eventually, Keir turned to me.

"I was just wondering," I began. "Your theory is based upon us all working off ancient memories, things from beyond a time we could have ever experienced, but in reality memories don't work like that. We make new memories every day, every hour, and they overlay the old ones, sometimes pushing them out. So why are there no new memories creating the same effect?"

Keir looked at me for a moment, perhaps wondering if I was trying to debunk his whole theory or seriously wondering about the matter. When he did speak, it was carefully measured.

"What I'm talking about," he said, "are core memories. Memories, like our childhood ones, that create the essence of who we are. Of course, there are newer memories, newer rituals, that are formed by modern life which also affect us. We don't talk about spells or magic in the same way these days, we don't believe in the power of symbolism like our ancestors did, but it's still there."

"Can you give me an example?" I pushed.

"Well, there's one that springs to mind," Keir replied. "Right here in Glasgow. I'm still looking into it, perhaps for another book, but..." He paused and then decided to go ahead anyway.

"I don't know how many of you know this, but the Subway system here opened in 1896 – and closed again almost immediately. Originally, the cars were cable hauled. By which I mean there was no electrified system, the carriages were hooked onto a continuously moving cable and this *dragged* them from station to station, the driver uncoupling from it when they arrived. However, on the first day of use, at 3pm exactly, a complete breakdown of the system occurred on the Outer Circle, meaning that passengers were forced to disembark and walk in the dark along the tracks to the nearest station. As a result of this, one man got his foot caught in the cable haul and it was almost torn off when the cable started moving unexpectedly.

"The system had only been open for ten hours and it had already tasted blood.

"But worse was to come as, eight hours later, a stationary carriage, awaiting clearance to approach St Enoch station, was hit by another train running at full speed. A total of 50 passengers were involved in this accident, 18 of whom were seriously injured." He paused. "It is said that there was also a death, but that the Subway company hushed it up, having enough bad press on their hands already. "

Keir looked out over his audience. They, and I, were entranced.

"Whatever the truth about the death, it is documented that a lot of the passengers involved in the crash had been riding the Subway for most of the day. Round and round. The fare at the time was one penny for as long as you wanted to travel and lots of people took advantage of the excitement of this new invention to do just that. They had been on the trains since the accident earlier on, constantly moving in a circle over tracks that had blood on them. Talking, laughing, breathing in the air of the subway – repeating the actions over and over. Like an incantation.

"And now, perhaps as a result of that, there was this new accident. More blood on the tracks. A sacrifice asked for and given, a thirst slaked.

"It is worth noting as well that, when the Subway had been built, the workers had reported strange noises underground, and sudden patches of great heat that would arrive from nowhere, making work impossible. One man likened it to a great beast breathing out."

Keir paused once more. "The Subway opened again the following year, with a revised fare system to avoid overcrowding and a better scheduling of trains. It was deemed a success, so much so that it's still in use today. It is rumoured, however, that before it re-opened certain experts were brought in to explore the tunnels. Experts in arcane matters. And certain precautions were also put into place.

"The revised schedule, for instance, made for a regularity that had not been there before, and the sigil for the Subway Company changed and was put on every carriage. Today, I am reliably told, it is still on the carriages, but underneath them, where no one can see, riding close to the rails. All of which turned the Subway into one giant binding spell, constantly repeated day after day. The motion of the Inner Circle counteracting and holding the energy that had been released in the Outer Circle. Death and bloodshed vanquished by the nourishing life brought by the passengers.

"Now, whether this is just an echo of an older ritual or a new one that has been created for a new age, I can't yet say. But it is, I would argue, proof that we all follow rituals and patterns, magic if you will, without actually realising it."

Keir pointed to another hand that was raised and moved on to another topic in his book – what part UFOs played in his theory – but I'd had enough. I excused myself to Susan and went outside for a cigarette. I didn't smoke often, perhaps once a week, but I suddenly felt as if I needed one.

The talk disturbed me that night, but less for its content and more for what I thought it might say about Susan. It was a whole side of her that I had never seen before and, when we got back to her apartment, I scoured her bookshelves for any further examples of this lunacy. Thankfully, other than possibly a couple of Stephen King books, I couldn't see anything.

In the days that followed, with studies starting to bite hard and the prospect of the Easter break looming, I forgot all about that evening. I travelled across the city by bus and by subway and, to be honest, the actions of some of the drivers on the roads scared me far more than the prospect of eldritch terrors in the tunnels beneath them. Life fell back into its usual pattern.

It must have been a couple of weeks after the talk that I found myself going home from Susan's flat and travelling on a very packed subway.

Normally, I would have stayed over, but I had an early lecture and I needed to get back to collect some papers for it. Regretfully, lingeringly, we said goodbye on the doorstep to her flats and I walked the five-minute path to Govan station.

No sooner had I gone through the sliding doors of the station than I knew there would be trouble ahead. A large sign in the foyer said INNER CIRCLE SUSPENDED. No explanation was given, just an offer to use the Outer Circle line for all stations instead. Great – so now, instead of travelling 5 stops to home, I had to go through ten.

I considered getting a bus, but at this time of night they were fairly infrequent in this area. I decided the best I could do was to catch the train and, if it was for any reason intolerable, get off at the next stop, Partick, where there was a much better chance of finding a bus home. I made my way through the barriers and over to the escalator.

When I reached the platform, it was pandemonium. A large group of youths, around 30 in total, all dressed in Santa costumes despite the time of year, were scattered along the waiting area. Evidently on the infamous Sub Crawl, they were no less annoying for my having recognised them as fellow students. My sigh was lost underneath the raucous cheering and catcalling filling the station platform.

I was about to walk further down the station in an effort to avoid them when the train pulled in. It was already almost full, so I made a dash for the nearest door, hoping to get in before the masses and therefore to at least be able to stand for my short journey. The state of my fellow travellers had made the decision for me that Partick would be my last stop.

I jumped in and a few others did likewise. There was a spot over by the opposite door where I could stand, crouched slightly under the curve of the carriage, and still hold on to a pole for safety. Further down the carriage, I could hear the Sub Crawl guys pushing their way in, their actions forcing more people to press up against me as the volume of passengers increased.

The doors closed and the train plunged into the darkness of the tunnel.

Even over the noise in the carriage I could hear the train itself, the rattle as it moved along the rails, the strange metallic scream that ululated through the carriage as it picked up speed. It shuddered as we moved, everyone's muscles tightening as we tried not to fall into each other with every lurch. The revellers were doing their best to drown everything out, but the Subway held them in its grip and not even they were immune to the shaking and rumbling surrounding them.

Suddenly, the train shuddered to a halt.

We were all thrown into one another. A large lady just in front of me suddenly careened into my shoulder and, as similar scenes played out through the carriage, muttered apologies could be heard everywhere. Then the lights went out.

Only briefly – a few seconds at most – but the effect was startling. Total darkness. Even the person closest to me was now invisible. And alongside the darkness, something seldom experienced on the subway. Silence. For those brief seconds, it was as if everything had been wiped out. There was no tunnel, no train. No passengers. Just myself, adrift in a darkened sea.

Then, with a flicker, the lights returned. There were a few sighs of relief but no other sounds. It was as if everyone, the revellers included, had experienced the same as me and it had left a small mark on all of us.

There was a groan from somewhere further down the carriage. Robbed of any of the usual noises associated with the train, it sounded closer than it actually was. I craned my head around the pole to see if I could see the cause.

Further down the carriage, towards the last set of doors, I saw someone slump over in their seat. Then, a second later, another figure, close by the first, also went limp and seemed to fall backwards into theirs. The people who were standing around them, in the aisles and by the doors, looked worried briefly and then they too went limp. Yet they remained standing. If they had been holding onto a support, the grip remained, but their bodies were evidently asleep.

I couldn't believe what I was seeing. I could see this wave of unconsciousness moving down the coach towards me, more and more people succumbing to a blackout similar to that the train had suffered only moments before. As it was getting closer, my heart started to pound and I realised that just ahead of this wave was another sensation.

Heat. It was like a warm pulse of some kind was getting closer, and as it passed each person on its journey, they yielded to sleep and oblivion. I turned to try the doors behind me, knowing that they would not open and that, even if they did, the tunnel walls were too close to allow me to escape – but I had to try something. The air was heating up around me. I could feel sweat on my brow but whether it was from the temperature or the situation I could not say.

I looked back from the doors just as a woman, sitting on the other side of the glass partition from me, slumped in her seat. I braced myself, and as I did so two other things happened.

The first was a sensation – nothing physical I could point to, but I was as sure of it as I am the words on this paper. I could feel something around me. Under me. It was like standing in a boat on the ocean and seeing the shadow of a whale pass beneath you. Something huge and alien and potentially dangerous was close by. I could sense it.

At the same time, my mind flashed back to the talk in the bookshop and a description Bernard Keir had related from the original builders of the subway tunnels. *Like a great beast breathing out.*

And then there was just darkness.

The next thing I remember, I was on the escalator coming up from the platform at Partick station. Other travellers were around me and I could hear the slight screech of the train pulling away on the tracks below me.

At the time, nothing seemed amiss. I didn't remember the train stopping, or the incidents that had happened straight after it. I had got on the train one stop earlier and travelled to this point just as I had intended.

It was later, days later, that the memories started to come back. At first, I thought I was remembering a dream, some bizarre night vision brought on by too many deep fried pakoras, but gradually I came to see it as more than that.

I found myself nervous, a tremor passing through my body, whenever I approached a subway station. At Govan, I would even describe it as a terror. My body didn't want to go back down there. When I did force myself, the roaring of the air past the sides of the carriages once we were in the tunnels started to sound more like the bellowing of an animal and I found that I couldn't complete my journey. In the end, my inability to travel more than a couple of stops without feeling acute fear meant that I gave up Subway travel altogether.

To this day, I don't know what really happened down there. In the tunnels. In the darkness. Would I have even remembered it if my mind had not already been primed by the talk in the bookshop?

I still don't know if I believe in Keir's ancient beasts theory, or that the operation of one railway line helps to contain whatever it is that moves on the other, but I know I felt something down there. And I know too that it wasn't just something passing by – it lived there and it was prowling. Hunting.

What I am sure of, though, is this. Whatever is down there didn't find what it was looking for – be it blood, sacrifice or something else – but it's still searching. And, for as long as I know that, I will never travel those lines again.

Subway
Notice
Due to football at Ibrox today
the Subway will be busier
than usual between
16:00-17:45 and 19:30-21:30
Thank you for your patience

Ibrox

I've never liked football.

It was a source of some embarrassment growing up. As a Manchester lad, you had only two choices – United or City. If you didn't play, at school, in the streets, you were weird, but if you didn't support one or the other, you were nothing. Your team gave you your identity.

For a while as a kid, I pretended to like Man City. Honestly, I think this was only because my brother-in-law supported United and I didn't really like him, but it got too much. I was supposed to know the latest score, who the players were, who the *opposing team's* players were – it was too much hard work for very little return. On top of that, it was almost impossible to tell who someone else supported, so when challenged I could proudly state City and still get my head kicked in for it. If I didn't support anybody, I'd also get beaten up, so why bother putting in the work?

I mean, it was just eleven men kicking a ball around on a field, trying to stop another eleven men from kicking it too. Where was the interest?

Anyway, I grew up, I moved away from Manchester. Football faded into the background, only resurfacing when the news reported the latest shockingly high transfer fee a player was getting.

Then I moved to Glasgow.

The thing about Glasgow is – and I love this city – you don't have to scratch far below its surface to find division, sectarianism. I was visiting the Tron one day, booking some theatre tickets not long after arriving here, when I heard a commotion from a nearby street. Naturally, I went to look. There was an Orange March going down Saltmarket.

Now, as a Manchester lad of a certain age, I was used to parades like this. We had Wakes Weeks when I was a kid – the equivalent of Fair Fortnight here, when all the factories shut and everyone went on holiday – and we had churches marching, banners flying, Trade Unions displaying, even Masons walking in the parades that started them off. But this was different. Here there was a definite Them and Us. Some of the people on the streets were cheering the March; others were ready to start a fight. The atmosphere was charged with potential violence. I got out of there pretty quick.

And it didn't take long to realise that this division had a very obvious, year-round figurehead, and that was football. Take United v City, add a dash of religious conflict, put it on steroids and you've got Rangers v Celtic.

Anyway, I have even less interest in religion than I have in football, so I didn't really think this would bother me at all. Avoid the Marches, avoid the matches, everything would be okay.

Except you can't in this city. I was walking into work one day and there was another March on, the bands and brightly-sashed participants all waiting along Sauchiehall Street for the start, stretching from the GFT to the Beresford. It was impressive and unavoidable. Going to the Barras one Saturday, for a mooch around the wonderful stalls, I realised that I was heading in the direction of Celtic's grounds. The streets and the pubs turned emerald and white around me, groups of men sang unfamiliar songs in the street. I felt like I'd trespassed on foreign ground.

So, when I got to Partick station one morning, on my way to see a friend in town, and I could hear raucous singing coming from the concourse, I nearly turned around and went back home. I'd travelled in by overground train from Clydebank that day – thinking back, I had noticed a couple of guys wearing Rangers scarfs a few seats down from me. But now, as I came down from the platform, I could see there were barriers up to marshal the crowds into some kind of order, there were police and rail security guys standing in huddles, and there was a small sea of blue and white filling the hallway. Rangers were definitely playing at home.

I knew my friend was coming from even further away than me and I couldn't really stand them up. I could catch a bus – but I'd only ever travelled on two buses since arriving in Glasgow and I had no idea how long it would take or even which route to get. It was going to have to be the subway.

At least Ibrox was only a few stops away and after that the train would be largely empty.

Most of the crowds seemed to be queueing for tickets, so I was able to make my way over to the barriers quite easily. Good start. Unfortunately, it went downhill from there.

The train was waiting for me when I got to the bottom of the escalator and, amazingly, it was quite quiet. There were only a few people on board, sitting patiently, waiting for the train to pull out. I joined them and I think we were all hoping for the doors to close and for the train to pull out before the hordes arrived from upstairs.

As time dragged on, however, it was obvious that wasn't going to happen. The train stayed stubbornly on the platform, doors open like some hungry beast awaiting its food. Then it was dinnertime.

A mass of people – mainly male, all patterned in blue and white – flowed down the escalators. They didn't ride down on the escalator, however; that was too slow. They ran down it, whooping and shouting to one another as they came. Straight onto the platform, straight in through the open doors.

The carriage filled up fast. All the seats were quickly taken and new people were forced to stand, filling the central walkway and spilling into the space by the doors. Still they came, pushing bodies even closer together. A sudden bang on the window opposite me made me jump. Someone trying to get the attention of someone in the carriage. A head was thrust in through the mass of people by the doorway –

"Hey, Georgie! Any seat by you?"

- a bizarre request, given the crush. A guy stood in front of me looked around, as if that would magically make an empty seat appear, then bellowed "Naw!" back at the door. I saw his eyes linger on me for a moment, almost a scowl on his face, then they flicked away.

The doors closed. It took two attempts as the taller guys beside them had to bend in to allow for the curvature of the roof, but then we were off. The whole carriage smelled of cheap body spray and bravado. The heat was suddenly oppressive.

We had entered the tunnel when two men, both in their late thirties I'd guess, started up a conversation. The problem here was that there were at least 7 or 8 people between them, so they were forced to shout across everyone. I didn't follow what was being said - something about a player, I guessed – but in the middle of it, without any warning at all, half the coach broke into song. It was an anthem of the terraces evidently, and it only lasted two lines, but somehow it fitted in to the rhythm of the shouted conversation perfectly, like the vocal version of a flash mob all suddenly dancing the same steps. It was, bizarrely, quite magical.

Then we were at Govan. The doors opened but, unsurprisingly, no one got out. There were a few people on the platform who wanted to get on but would evidently have to wait for the next train. With very little pause, the doors slid together again and the train started up, but not before I heard a chilling announcement over the intercom.

"This train," it said, "will terminate at Ibrox. All passengers must disembark at Ibrox."

I'm sure the voice repeated the message, but I couldn't hear it if he did. Loud cheers at the second mention of Ibrox drowned out all other information.

The noise and the heat continued all the way to the next station. I didn't feel like part of it, so for the most part I kept my eyes down and studied the shoes of those around me. When I did lift my eyes up, however, I noticed the same guy from earlier – Georgie - looking at me again. I didn't want to make eye contact, because there was something confrontational in his gaze, but I had to look again.

Now he was talking to another man next to him. Then Georgie nudged him and nodded his head in my direction. The other man looked and this time there was a definite scowl from him, directed at me. I looked down again, unsure of what else to do.

As the train pulled into the station, however, the new guy decided to take matters into his own hands.

"Whit the fuck is youse doin' on here?" he said, stabbing a finger towards me.

"I... I'm just," I started but I didn't know what to say. I was on a train, same as him – what did he think I was doing?

"Fenian!" he spat at me and jabbed his finger in my chest.

I was shocked and looked down at where he had poked, as if that would explain things.

As it turned out, it did.

I was looking down at my t-shirt. My fashionably bright green t-shirt. Suddenly, it made sense.

"No," I said. "You've got it wrong. I don't support anybody. Not Rangers or..." I let it hang in the air, not sure what the response would be for mentioning the Hated Opponents' name in this company.

By this time, the train had stopped and people were starting to get off.

Georgie decided to get in on the conversation first, though. "The Gers not good enough for yeh, aye?"

I was going to answer back, but suddenly I was ten years old again. I knew that it didn't matter what reply I gave it would be the wrong one. As far as the bullies were concerned, my fate was sealed. God, I hated football.

"Look, I'm getting off," I said, making it sound like a decision, a choice.

Georgie looked back at his mate and sniffed. A look passed between them but I was already on my feet, pushing ahead of them. I didn't get very far – the crush of people in the carriage was too much to make a bolt for it – but I did manage to put at least two bodies between me and them. That would have to do for the moment.

As I got closer to the doors, I hoped that the increased space would give me chance to get away, but if anything, it got worse. There was a momentary pause on the threshold of the doors that allowed me time to tug the zipper of my jacket closed, hiding the offending colour from any other troublesome eyes, and then I was propelled onto the platform.

It felt like I had been swallowed whole by some great beast. I know that sounds fanciful and probably some of you reading this will be rolling your eyes, but it was the only way I could describe it. There were no people here – yes, faces bobbed up and down in the melee, but they seemed less like individuals and more like a shifting pattern. The sheer *weight* of the crowd was all around me, a force of gravity that pulled me along with it. I had not intended to go up the stairs – if I had formulated anything like a plan it was to stand aside once I left the train and let my pursuers rush past like villains in some cartoon – but here I was being propelled towards the steps.

There was no chance to turn back. The momentum of the crowd was to get out of the station and I, like flotsam on a tide (or food being swallowed whole), had no choice but to go along with them.

I had never been to Ibrox station before and the winding route of the stairs was a challenge for me. The pressure of the crowd was all around me. I turned at their whim. At one point, my foot slipped on a step and I had a momentary vision of falling to the floor, hundreds of feet trampling across me before the crowd even realised I was there. Thankfully, I recovered my balance.

Suddenly, I could see daylight ahead of me. Not direct, but proving that there was a way out from this crush of people. Another corner was turned and then, before I knew it, I was at the turnstiles. People flowed past me on either side, tapping their cards or tickets and pushing through before the barriers had even closed again. I dug into my pocket and pulled out my own card, pushing it to the reader and then bolting out for the sun.

Once out onto the street, the crowd relaxed its grip as people began to disperse. Some flowed over to the squat pub across the road – the Louden Tavern, proudly proclaiming itself The Quintessential Rangers Supporters Pub. A phalanx of bouncers was clearly visible by its doors, black-clad and implacable amidst the blue tide swirling round them.

For my part, my first reaction was to stand and take in the scene before me. I realised I was suddenly very cold. The day was not particularly chilly but suddenly standing on my own, outside and without the pressurised body heat of the crowd, made the afternoon seem colder than it was. I pulled my thin jacket closer around me.

I noticed with some relief that most of the crowd was moving away from me. I knew that the Ibrox Stadium was somewhere over to the right of the station – even though I couldn't see it, the crowd was headed in that rough direction, like migrating birds. Between it and me, however, there was a whole new world.

The street the subway emptied onto, Copland Street, was awash with people. Notionally, there was a road down the middle of it, but I pitied the driver that tried to get past the hordes filling the tarmac. The noise was incredible – singing, shouting, whistles, filling the air and creating a soundtrack of pure confusion. Competing with this came the smells. Not the crush of the crowd smell from the subway; here it was the fragrance of burger vans. Grilled meat and fried onions assaulted my nose, familiar and slightly nauseating at the same time.

There was a carnival atmosphere in the air. There were even side shows in the form of the brightly coloured stalls selling yet more scarfs or bobble hats, flags and t-shirts. The hawkers called out to anyone passing, adding to the chaos of the street. The ground was littered with empty Buckfast bottles, clinking occasionally as someone kicked one against a curb.

As I looked, I also noticed another colour coming to the fore in the mix – yellow. This I realised with some relief was the colour of the police. The more I looked, the more of them I could see, and then suddenly I heard a new sound – the clopping of hooves – and turned to see two mounted police men approaching on horseback.

I had lost track of my potential aggressors in the crowd coming up from the platform, but the sheer bulk of the horses, alongside their riders towering over the crowd as they passed, gave me comfort. If they were to try anything now, there would be protection nearby. The horses passed, the crowd parting to let them through.

I wanted to go back into the station but decided to give it a few minutes. I moved around to the other side of the station, a quiet suburban street that seemed a world away from the mass of bodies just around the corner. I considered walking to the next subway station, but realised that I didn't know which way to go. In the end, I settled for texting my friend to tell them I was running late.

Standing there, waiting for the chance to slip back inside the station, I couldn't help but reflect on the events of my day so far. Football had, whether I liked it or not, been a part of my life for longer than I cared to admit. It was always there in the background, even though I had chosen to keep it there. Not so much a guilty pleasure, more a hidden dirty secret. Something I didn't want to acknowledge in my life. Today had done nothing to change that opinion.

I took a deep breath and turned the corner. The crowd was smaller now, further away. I dived back into the subway and determined to get as far away from Ibrox as I could.

I've never liked football and today I'd learned that football didn't like me.

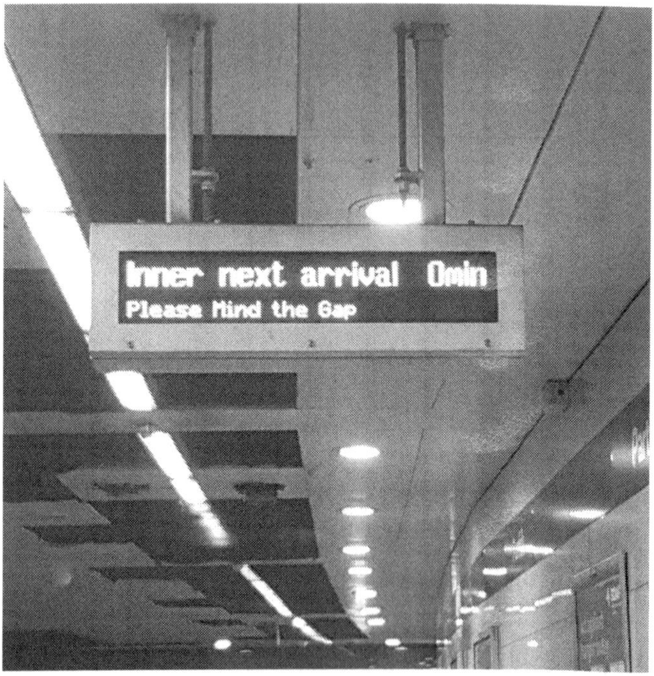
Inner next arrival 0min
Please Mind the Gap

Cessnock

Rory looked down at the rails and they glinted back at him like a blade.

He sat on the stairs, one foot on the platform, the other one step up, as if his whole body was unwilling to make the commitment. There were only two other people at Cessnock station, each further down the central platform, one facing the Inner Line, the other facing the Outer. All waiting for a train.

The signal told him that the Outer Line would arrive first. He realised he was sat closer to the Inner's side but it wasn't a preference. Rory looked over to the rails again.

The subway had been there all his life. For the amount of people they had carried, for the burden of all those trains, the rails showed no sign of wear. Parts of them, buffed by the constant transit of wheels over them, shone under the electric lights, whereas other sections looked dull and grey. Rory felt as if he could feel the solidity of them, the permanence. It was cold and uncaring.

For the fifth time that hour, he checked his phone. No messages. He hadn't really expected any –

his head knew that she was not going to reply to him, but his foolish heart kept hoping. She hadn't replied for two days. There was no reason to think she would now.

Without even thinking about it, Rory's fingers flicked across the screen and brought up his Gallery. A bank of tiny thumbnails showed him happier times. Elaine smiling to camera, Elaine laying her head on his shoulder, Elaine blowing him a kiss. His thumb jabbed out and made one of the pictures fill the screen.

It had been taken only a few weeks ago. They had been shopping in Partick – Elaine loved to wander around Charity Shops looking for bargains and that area of town had plenty. She was posing, Insta-style, with a blouse she had found. He remembered that she had asked him to take the picture so that she could post it later. Rory couldn't remember if he had sent it over to her in the end or not. He considered doing it now – an olive branch – but wondered if it would just seem creepy.

He looked at the picture until the screen darkened and winked out.

Mickey noticed the young man sat on the stairs but paid him no attention. He was stood at the far end of the same platform, waiting for the Inner line to arrive, waiting for the chance to get to Buchanan Street and the fresh air and the opportunity to light up a ciggie.

He had always found the subway slightly claustrophobic. Oddly, it wasn't the carriages that did it, it was the buildings. The knowledge that you were underground, below the streets - the only way in or out via a staircase or escalators. Or through the dark and deepening tunnels. There were times when he could feel the weight of the streets above him, pushing down, only the curve of the ceiling giving him hope that the structure was safe.

It was daft, he knew it, but on days like this it hit him hard and he had to muster all his strength to stay on the platform and not to rush past the young man, back to the surface.

Mickey's fingers played with the ready-rolled cigarette in his jacket pocket and unconsciously he licked his bottom lip, ready to put the paper to it.

Mickey was an old school smoker. He rolled his own, not even bothering with a filter. His wife – God rest her soul – had always said it would be the death of him, but in the end that great sneering bastard in the sky had chosen to take her first, even though she'd never smoked a day in her life. That had been three years ago and, even though Mickey had flirted with the idea of vapes and even bought commercial packets over the counter, he'd gone back to rolling his own. Arthritis or some such ailment was starting to move around his body and Mickey found it difficult sometimes to pull on his trousers in a morning or reach for a tin on a high shelf, but his fingers – yellowed and callused – were still as nimble as ever in making his roll-ups. Muscle memory, he thought it was. He didn't even have to look at what they were doing.

Mickey looked up and saw that the Outer Line was about to arrive. He took in a deep breath and let it out again as a wet phlegmy cough that echoed off the walls of the station.

Marie looked over at the poster on the walls of the tunnel and wished that she had a life like that.

It was for a theatre production, an opera. Brightly coloured people wearing fashionable clothes and sporting smiles broader than a toothpaste commercial posed artfully in the image. There was a party going on, alcohol flowed freely. No one had a care in the world. Jaunty letters proclaimed it *The Marriage Of Figaro*.

Although the party looked fun, that wasn't what Marie wanted. She just wanted to go to the opera. Any opera.

The other day, on her way down Sauchiehall Street, she had heard a young girl singing. Probably a student of the Conservatoire one street over, she was stood outside the empty carcase of Marks & Spencer's, a microphone on a stand in front of her and a large speaker beside her. The music must have been on tape, but the voice was all her own.

Marie had no idea what the song was, but she guessed it was from an opera. Words she couldn't understand flowed out of the tiny figure before her, twisting and rising in the air like butterflies floating on a breeze. The song soared so that it filled the street around her, echoing up and down the way and pulling people to it. It spoke of a yearning, a longing – for love and for life – that called to every single person there. In the middle of a grey shopping street, amongst the vape shops and coffee houses, it promised something more. Something special.

Marie had stood entranced as the young girl finished her song. Then a polite smattering of applause broke the spell and people started to move away again. Marie felt as if a part of her had moved away with them. The young girl had looked hopefully for anyone putting money in her collecting hat, but no one took a step towards it.

Now, looking at a poster on a subway wall, Marie realised she had only been to the theatre three times in her life, twice for panto and once as part of a Hen Party to a version of *The Bodyguard*. All three visits had been to the King's Theatre and she had been struck every time by the extravagance of the building. The foyer with its painted and plaster-worked ceiling, the statues of two naked women that flanked the stained glass windows, the marble on the staircase and walls. Even before she stepped into the darkened auditorium, with its flowing lines around the different levels and painted cherubs, with the stage curtains so big she had to tip her head back to see the top, it had been a magical place. A place she simultaneously felt at home in and knew was not for her.

She moved the bag she was carrying from one hand to the other, feeling the heft of the cleaning supplies within it. The people whose houses she cleaned, they were the ones that went to the theatre. They would go to operas. People like Marie didn't feature in plays on the stage, bringing up three children, holding down two jobs. Mozart never wrote operas about the wife of a van driver. This was her life, here. On the outside looking in.

A loud cough brought her back from her thoughts. The old man who had winked at her as he had walked down the platform must have made the noise. She glanced over and he was wiping his mouth on the back of his sleeve. Marie looked away again before she caught his eye.

Rory watched as the train for the Outer Line pulled into the station. The woman who had been waiting for it got on and the doors closed. A handful of passengers wandered towards the steps as the train pulled out again.

Rory pulled himself in towards the handrail as the new arrivals pushed past him. He didn't try to get up as there was plenty of room to get by, but even so he heard a few tuts and sighs as people were forced to queue behind one another to get through the space. He didn't look up at any point. If he was a disappointment to them, it was only because he had been a disappointment to everyone in his life.

His therapist had referred to Rory's depression as his Black Dog. Then he'd shown him a short cartoon on YouTube that explained, in a humorous way, how to live with it. Rory liked the cartoon but he didn't think it would do any good. When his depression hit, it wasn't anything as friendly as a dog. It was a wolf, a snarling savage beast that tore his self-confidence apart and shredded his world into unidentifiable bits.

It had stolen his sleep and his appetite, led to arguments with his family and, ultimately, it had taken Elaine from him. He'd tried medication but it left him feeling less than himself, numbed and diminished, so he had stopped taking it. He had no one to blame but himself for where he was in life, he knew that – but the wolf knew it too and in the corners of his mind it was always there to remind him.

Rory looked down at the tracks again and wondered if anyone would actually miss him. At the end of his therapy sessions, the therapist would always ask the same question: "Do you have thoughts of self-harm or suicide?" The answer had always been no, but the wolf had heard the question too and had worried at it like the bloodied corpse of a rabbit. *It's an option*, the wolf told him. *It's here waiting for you. It's what they expect of you. Why not give it to them?*

When he had come down the steps to the platform, Rory hadn't been sure if that was what he wanted or not. He wasn't going anywhere, there was no other reason for him to be on the platform, but part of his brain told him that just being there would show him the error of his thoughts, turn him away from that path. Instead, it had brought it into focus.

Rory checked his phone one more time. Still no messages.

A faint rumbling noise and a slight push of cold air told him that the train was coming. Rory put his phone down on the step beside him. Not so much a goodbye note, more a memory of him. All his life was in that phone if someone wanted to find it, wanted to find out who he was. Had been.

Then he stood up, putting both feet now on the tiled floor. He took one step away from the stairs, so that he was on the edge of the platform, beyond the line of raised dots that marked the safe place to stand. Rory took a deep breath and closed his eyes. The train was here. He could hear the brakes being applied to slow it down. They sounded like a wolf howling.

Mickey glanced up at the illuminated sign and saw that the train's status had changed to 'Approaching'. His fingers played with the cigarette in his pocket again and he felt a tiny straw of tobacco come loose. He rubbed it between his fingers, then brought them up to his nose. Not long now until he could light up.

Now that the woman had gone, he wondered if he should move further up the platform. The rear carriage of her train, when it had stopped opposite him, had been quite busy but the central coach was quieter. Perhaps it was worth him moving to that position.

As he walked up the platform, he glanced over at the only other person there, the lad on the steps. He was standing up now. No doubt he'd also seen the sign change. Mickey was about to take his own position when he spotted something else.

"Hey, pal," he said. "You've left your phone on the stairs."

The noise of the approaching train took his words and threw them away. The boy didn't seem to have noticed. Mickey could see the tunnel beside the figure starting to get lighter as the train approached.

He walked towards the boy. "Hey, pal. Pal!"

Now that he was closer to him, Mickey could see that the boy had his eyes closed. Which was odd. Not really knowing what was happening, Mickey moved a little faster towards him.

The train was almost at the end of the tunnel when Mickey reached the boy.

"Hey pal," he said again. The boy opened his eyes and turned to face him just as the train came out of the tunnel. They were both so close to the edge of the platform that the wind from its arrival knocked them slightly off balance and Mickey instinctively put an arm out to steady the boy away from the edge.

The boy looked down at it and then over to him. For a brief second, Mickey thought he saw anger in his eyes, pure and almost animal, but then it passed. It was replaced with confusion.

"Is everything alright, lad?" Mickey asked. "You almost forgot your phone there." He pointed to the steps behind them.

The lad looked at him for what seemed like a long moment. The train stopped beside them and the doors to the carriages opened, but neither man paid them any attention.

"Yeah, yeah, I'm fine," the young man said. His voice was distant and he looked as if he was waking from a dream. "Thank you."

"Best pick it up before it gets trampled," Mickey said. The young man blinked and then turned to get his phone.

"Good thing I saw it," Mickey continued. "Anyway, the train's here now. Should we get on it?"

The boy turned back to him. It looked to Mickey like the lad was truly seeing him for the first time. "No", he said. "I, er, I've remembered something I have to... I'm not getting this."

Some passengers had reached the steps and were pushing past the two of them to get out.

Mickey frowned for a second. "Aye, alright. Well, anyway, I'll be getting it. Have a good day."

The young man looked at him and then, surprisingly, stuck out his hand. Mickey was slightly confused by the gesture but nonetheless took the hand and shook it before dashing off for the closest doors. He just got into the carriage as they shut behind him.

As he sat down, he felt his chest tighten from the sudden exertion. Mickey grabbed a handkerchief out of his pocket and held it to his mouth as he was suddenly wracked with a deep hacking cough. He dimly noticed people in the carriage looking over at him, but the coughs were too violent to hide. The train was starting to pull away as he pulled the hankie away from his mouth. He sneaked a look at the contents. A blob of grey phlegm, spotted with red.

Probably not long now, he thought. I'll leave this world not having had an effect on anybody or anything.

Lost in his thoughts, he missed seeing the young man head back up the subway stairs, towards the light of the day above.

Priority seat
Please offer this seat to those less able to stand

Kinning Park

The playground was quiet, but then it usually was this early in the day. Fiona looked up at the climbing frame fort, the swings, the slide polished into shining brilliance by the trouser seats of hundreds of kids and thought about how sad it all looked without anyone to use it. Not that Daniel minded. For him, having the playground to himself was a bonus, a magic kingdom presided over by a six-year-old king.

Fiona envied her son's imagination. She watched him climbing the metal stepladder up to the fort's highest level, turning occasionally to fight off make-believe attackers and waving an invisible sword in triumph when he reached the top. He didn't hear the dull roar of the motorway nearby, didn't see the squat entrance to the Subway station. Daniel had always been better at being on his own than she had.

"Be careful," she called out to him as he fought off an imaginary foe by the edge of the slide. If Daniel heard her, he didn't let it disturb his furious battle, but he did step away from the drop slightly.

Fiona felt the insistent buzz of the phone in her pocket, but she ignored it. It would only be Catriona again, for the third time that morning. It wasn't as if her boss didn't know that Fiona started at midday, that this was one of the few chances she had to spend time with Daniel – why did she have to ring now? Experience told Fiona that it would be nothing important. Sod her. She'd ring back later.

A breeze caught Fiona's hair and tugged a strand across her eyes. She pushed it back into place absentmindedly as she looked across the park. She knew that Daniel didn't mind it, but she wished she had the money to take him somewhere nice. An indoor play group, a soft play centre, somewhere that he might meet other kids. Kinning Park was a little piece of green that they could escape to, away from the confines of the flat, but the winter was coming on and it wouldn't be long before it would be too cold to come here.

It didn't help that Jim was able to take Daniel to better places. Last weekend, when he'd had Daniel and Fiona had been working, the two of them had gone to the cinema at the Quay, then had a burger after. Daniel had talked about it all night before Fiona, tired and fighting off her anger, told him to go to bed.

It wasn't her son's fault. She knew that and she cursed herself for the times Daniel got to see the version of herself that seemed to have taken over lately. Fiona was aware her real anger was directed at Jim – had been since he'd walked out six months before. She had been livid then; furious at his excuses, at his insistence that there was no one else, that they had grown apart, that he needed space, that the flat was too small, their lives were too small. But, over time, this anger had solidified into something more, so that it was now a part of her being that she just couldn't let go of. Fiona felt as if she was being held prisoner by her fury – her old self looking out, helplessly, as a new and bitter Fiona took over her life.

It hadn't always been like that. When she and Jim had first moved into the flat that backed onto Kinning Park, life had seemed wonderful. Daniel was three years old and full of curiosity about the new place. Jim had recently had a promotion and the extra money was helping to pay for the larger flat, giving Daniel his own room for the first time. Fiona was working, but the extra money also allowed them childcare. Everything seemed good.

Then, as the months became years and Jim's second promotion fell away like autumn leaves, things started to change. Jim still doted over Daniel, she could see that, but he seemed to be falling out of love with her. They touched less, kisses grew more infrequent and she always seemed to be the one wanting them. They no longer slept curled up together, Jim preferring to pull away and move to a colder patch of the bed.

At first, she thought he was having an affair. It seemed to be the only explanation, but Fiona could find no evidence. Yes, he stayed late at work – but when she rang him, he was always at his desk. Yes, he went out with his friends more often, finding reasons to not be with her – but their wives and girlfriends backed up the stories he brought back. Fiona tried to suggest that they go out together, start a date night habit, but Jim never seemed interested. For a brief while, she even wondered if he was gay, but nothing suggested that either.

In the end, she just had to accept that he no longer wanted to be with her. She didn't know what she had done but she was willing to try anything to get him back. So, one night, after putting Daniel to bed, Fiona asked Jim what was wrong.

She had expected him to be surprised, for the question to open his eyes to how he had been acting over the last few months, but instead she was the one surprised. He thanked her for noticing, for giving him the opportunity to say something, and then he left her.

A tiny part of her, screaming in the core of her anger, wondered if he'd still be there if she hadn't asked.

The phone buzzed in her pocket again. "For fuck's sake, Rina," she muttered. "Just leave me alone."

After Jim left, things changed again. First, she had to explain it to Daniel (when in truth she had not really understood the reasons herself). Then she had to get used to the idea of being a single parent. Jim agreed to pay the rent on the flat, but all the other bills were hers. Part time work wasn't enough – Fiona realised she would have to go full time.

For a short while, her mother came down from Auchtermuchty, all flapping hands and hidden recriminations. She never said it, but Fiona could feel her evaluating her daughter to find what she had done to lose her husband. All the same, it allowed Fiona some space to negotiate extra hours at work and look for ways to have Daniel cared for while she was out; then, after a month, she was on her own again.

Something wet against her ankle pulled Fiona back to the present. She looked down and a small black West Highland Terrier was sniffing at the ground by the side of her. Its nose must have touched her exposed skin. She was about to shoo it away when she noticed the owner strolling across to the playground from the other side of the park. He had a small boy, around Daniel's age by the looks of it, with him, so she decided to leave the dog to his sniffing rather than cause trouble.

"Rab! Come here," the man shouted and the dog looked up. It looked back at Fiona for a moment, as if giving her chance to challenge the command, and then ambled off to see why it was needed.

The man and his son arrived at the climbing frame. Fiona glanced over at Daniel but he was too engrossed in his own world to notice the new arrivals.

The phone buzzed in her pocket once again and without thinking about it, Fiona pulled it out and answered it.

As expected, it was Catriona.

"Fiona. At last! I've been trying to get you all morning. I was wondering if you could start a bit early today. Say 11 o'clock rather than 12"

Even over the sound of the motorway behind her, Fiona could hear a stridency in Rina's voice that rubbed her up the wrong way.

"I'm sorry, Rina" she began, but her boss cut in.

"It's just that Madelle needs to get away early because she's got a doctor's appointment, and we can't leave the client on his own."

"I understand that," Fiona said, "but I've got Daniel and I can't drop him off at the daycentre until eleven, and I've got to get over there by subway…"

"Can't someone else drop him off?" Rina said.

Fiona bit back telling her that if she had someone else to see to Daniel, she wouldn't need the sitter at all. Catriona knew her situation, and knew that it would change soon when the school year started up again – why did she have to be so insensitive?

"No," Fiona said, carefully. "And this is also one of the few mornings I get to spend with him, so I'm not cutting it short."

"Well, if that's your attitude," Rina began, but Fiona had heard enough.

"It's not my attitude, it's my right, Catriona" she snapped. "You set the rota three weeks ago and I have arranged my life around it. This is my time now. I'm back on your clock at twelve, so either Madelle will have to make another appointment on *her* time or you will have to cover for an hour."

There was a silence at the other end of the phone. Then Rina came back on, voice as cold as the iron holding the playground swings.

"I'll see you at twelve, then. When I hand the client over to you."

The phone went dead. Fiona knew that she would be walking into trouble later. She was in the right, but Rina was notoriously bad with her staff. She rang them on holiday, swapped shifts with little or no notice, and generally treated everyone like dogsbodies. Fiona knew there was a high turnover in carers under her but in some ways that didn't help – there *always* was a high turnover in the care sector, and there were more than enough candidates to fill the vacant posts. She was aware that Catriona only got away with her attitude because she didn't need to hold onto staff.

"Everything alright?" said a voice next to her.

Fiona looked up to see the man who had been calling his dog now stood in front of her.

"You looked a bit agitated," he said, and Fiona realised that she had probably raised her voice at the end of the call, Angry Fiona surfacing briefly.

"I know it's none of my business," the man continued. "I'm sorry if I intruded."

Fiona looked at him. Crossing the park, he'd been just a generic male figure, with a young boy and a dog. Up close, she noticed that he was of Middle Eastern origin, although the accent suggested he was at least second-generation Glaswegian. He had dark hair and a generally well-groomed appearance about him. The man was starting to turn away.

"No," Fiona said. "No, it's alright. I... er, thank you."

The man smiled. "Well, our boys seem to be getting on alright, so I just thought..." His voice tailed off as if he wasn't quite sure how to end the sentence.

Fiona was briefly confused but then she looked past the man to the climbing frame. Daniel was no longer fighting imaginary foes; he was sat, cross-legged, on the top of the fort, talking animatedly to a young boy.

"Sameer doesn't tend to get on well with strangers," the man said. His eyes kept darting from the climbing frame to Fiona and back again, wanting to keep an eye on the boy yet not wanting to appear rude.

"Daniel is..." She wanted to say he was the same, but in truth she didn't know. She didn't see him with other children very often, and Fiona suddenly realised that she didn't know if her son was distanced or outgoing in the company of others.

"Sorry, I tend to prattle on a bit when I'm nervous. Terrible habit," the man was saying. "I'm Usman, by the way."

"Fiona," she replied and motioned that he should perhaps sit down on the bench beside her. "Easier to keep an eye on them."

Usman smiled. It was a warm, genuine smile – not like the ones she gave to the clients, not like the harsh brittle smiles she got from Catriona just before bad news was delivered, not like the slightly pitying smiles her mother had doled out. It took her slightly off guard.

"That's Daniel," she said, and then suddenly realised that she had already said her son's name. She felt herself flush and looked down at the pathway.

If Usman noticed the mistake, he didn't draw attention to it. They sat in silence for a moment, neither sure what to say next.

"Are you local?" Usman asked. "To here. To the park, I mean. I'm sorry, that's probably not something I should ask."

Fiona smiled. "No, it's okay. We live over there." She gestured broadly in the direction of their flat. *Her* flat.

"Nice," Usman said, not really taking his eyes off his son. "I have a shop over that way. We live in Newton Mearns, but Sameer likes to come in with me some days. Otherwise, he spends most of his time with his teta."

"Well, it gives his Mum a day off, I suppose," said Fiona. "For him to spend time with his father."

Usman looked at her for a moment and Fiona was suddenly aware that she must have made a mistake somehow.

"My fault," Usman said. "I apologise. Sameer spends most of the time with his *grandmother*. His mother died just after he was born."

"Oh, I'm sorry," Fiona stuttered, but Usman cut in.

"It's okay. How were you to have known? Sometimes I think it's better that he has no memory of her, that it's less painful for him. But a boy needs a mother and a father, like your Daniel, and I'm sorry he doesn't have that."

"Daniel's father and I are... separated," Fiona said, and now Usman was looking embarrassed. "It's okay," she continued. "You weren't to know either."

They shared a smile, each recognising a tinge of sadness behind the eyes of the other person, and then sat in silence for a few moments. The sound of the boys happily chattering away together drifted across to them, the words indistinct but the companionship evident. Rab the terrier sniffed around at the ground below the boys' platform, occasionally glancing up to make sure they were still there.

Fiona glanced at her watch. She would need to be going soon, catching the subway over to St George's Cross so that she could drop Daniel off before she went in to work. The thought of meeting Catriona at the handover of the client brought her anger forward again and at the same time Fiona realised that, at least for a few minutes, sitting in a park with a stranger, she had been more like her old self. She had almost forgotten what that was like.

"I, er, we have to be going soon," she said to Usman. "Sorry – I have work and I have to take Daniel over to a sitter for the day."

"Of course," the man replied. "Of course." He started to stand up.

"I just wondered if... If you were at this park the same time every Tuesday?" Fiona found herself saying. "I think it would be nice – for the boys – if they could meet up again."

Usman regarded her for a second. His eyes were kind. "That would be good, yes," he said. "For the boys. I should be able to get away."

Fiona smiled, awakening muscles she didn't feel as if she had used for some time.

They both called their sons over to them, Usman giving her a little wink as the boys groaned in unison at their time being up. Rab shuffled over to them and then spent a few minutes wandering between the dawdling boys and the adults, trapped between a world of freedom and one of duty. Eventually, everyone was ready and the boys said goodbye to one another as the adults vowed to meet again.

Fiona and Daniel walked off together towards the subway station, the path curving away from the playground so that it vanished from view. Usman and Sameer would have been out of sight even before that, strolling off to the far corner of the park, but Fiona didn't want to look back anyway.

As she passed through the ticket barriers into the subway, acknowledging silently that she was now heading into work and probably a confrontation with Rina, Angry Fiona reared up again, filling her head with arguments and self-doubt. This time, however, there was a difference. The fury was still there, but there was also something else, at the back of her mind, something that might one day blossom into hope.

It wasn't a lot but, for now, it was enough.

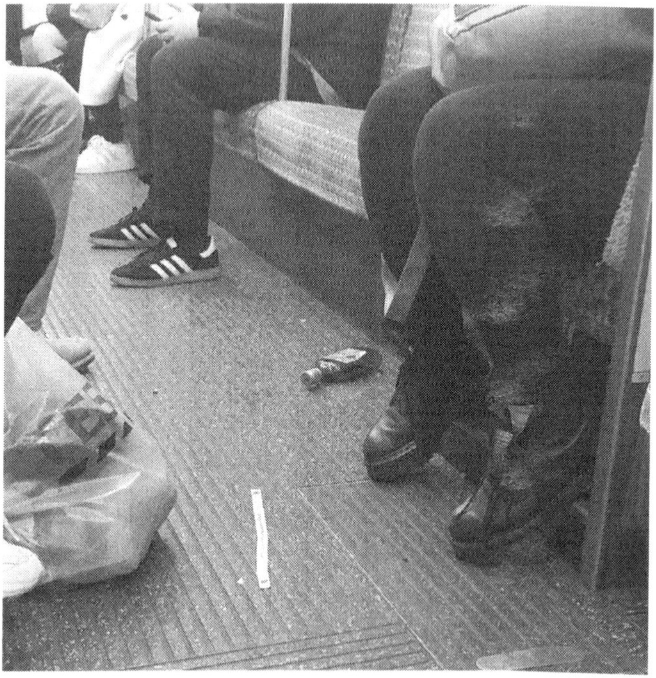

Shields Road

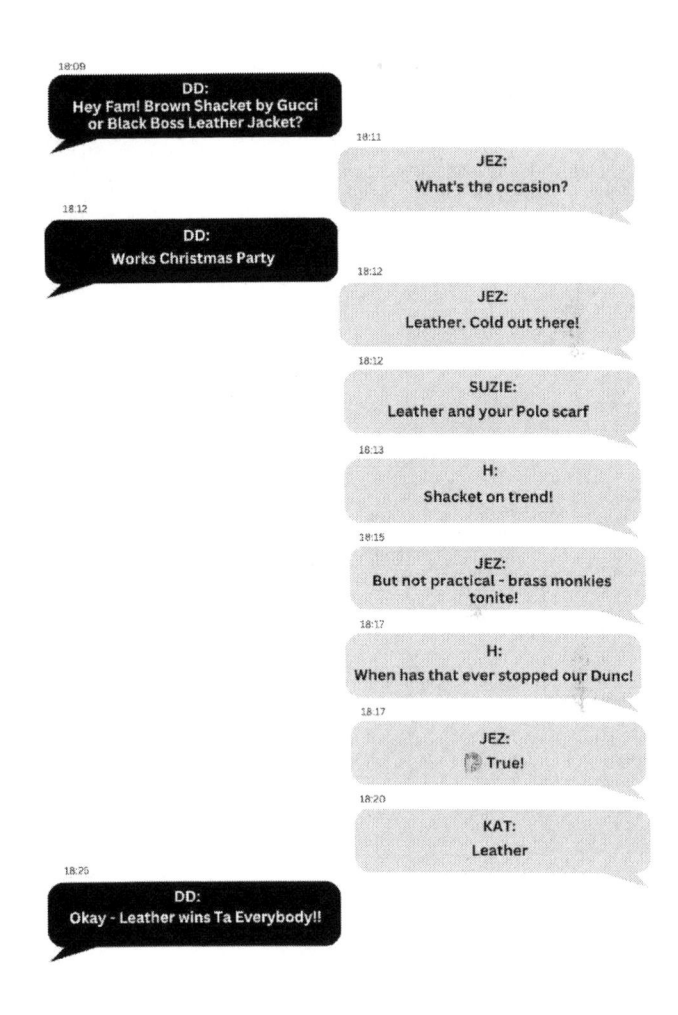

18:09 DD: Hey Fam! Brown Shacket by Gucci or Black Boss Leather Jacket?

18:11 JEZ: What's the occasion?

18:12 DD: Works Christmas Party

18:12 JEZ: Leather. Cold out there!

18:12 SUZIE: Leather and your Polo scarf

18:13 H: Shacket on trend!

18:15 JEZ: But not practical - brass monkies tonite!

18:17 H: When has that ever stopped our Dunc!

18:17 JEZ: 🍾 True!

18:20 KAT: Leather

18:26 DD: Okay - Leather wins Ta Everybody!!

18:25

JEZ:
You going in the Boxter? #PorscheBoy

18:26

DD:
No - want to have a few bevvies!

18:26

SUZIE:
Have a good night but be careful!

18:27

DD:
Always! Gotta go or will miss subway

18:40

DrunkenDuncan
Albert Drive, Pollokshields

No Internet. Picture will load when signal returns

DrunkenDuncan Looking fine on Subway platform! Heading into town for Xmas Bash! Look out Glasgow - the HAG is on his way!
#fashionvictim #TedBaker #Prada #Gucci #Burberry #youngfreeandsingle #YOLO

Journal
V2.23

Sat 21 Dec

Quote of the Day:

OPPORTUNITIES DON'T JUST HAPPEN
You Create Them!

Today's Entry:

What a day! Supposed to be my day off from work but of course Dad wants me to help out in the supermarket because it's the Saturday before Christmas and all the Chinese restaurants in Glasgow need their supplies... totally knackered now!

Then I had to get from Kelvinhall to Shields Road (thank you Subway - although next time can we not have a football match on at the same time, bloody Rangers fans! lol), then a 15 min walk to home in the freezing cold, get showered, spray on the Chanel Blue, get dressed and get out for another freezing 15 min walk and now here I am finally on the Underground to town!

Should be a good nite though. Us IT guys know how to party - bring it on!!!

Today I'm feeling:

TO DO:

18:59 JOHN: Yo, DD - wot time u arriving?

19:01 DD: Just out Subway. Be there for 1/4 past? U?

19:01 JOHN: Running late - not left house yet lol

19:02 DD: Lightweight!

19:02 JOHN: U tanked up already?

19:02 DD: No - just had a couple Peronis at home.

19:03 JOHN: Good man! I'm pure buzzin for tonite

19:04 DD: Me too! Don't forget your invite

19:04 JOHN: On my phone already. Don't have too much fun before i get there, lol

19:03 DD: Then get a move on!

19:07 JOHN: C U There!

VENTNER & HOGG
I T CONSULTANCY

INVITE YOU TO THEIR

CHRISTMAS PARTY!

Saturday 21st December
Browns Brasserie and Bar from 8pm

QR Code necessary for entrance to Private Bar

19:55 - 21:25

DrunkenDuncan
George Square, Glasgow

DrunkenDuncan Let's get this party started!!!
#ChristmasParty #ProseccoNight #OutOnTheTown #Youngfreeandsingle #YOLO
View all 16 Comments

DrunkenDuncan Network Engineering Dept in the house!! These guys are my work fam - John, Sheila, Jaiminee & Ahmed let's go!
#PrivateBar #BestNightEver #KillingIt #Christmas #Youngfreeandsingle #YOLO
View all 8 Comments
GovanGuy A likely looking bunch!

DrunkenDuncan Who'd have thought the boss spruced up so well? 😊
#SilverFox #OverFiftyAndFabulous #DILF #JustJoking #NotJoking #Youngfreeandsingle #YOLO
View all 6 Comments

21:54

JOHN:
Fuuuukk! Duncs just kissed the boss!

21:55

JEZ:
What?! Where?!

21:56

SUZIE:
Which Boss?

21:57

JOHN:
Just now at the party - Alan Hogg, one of the bif bosses! Dunc's pretty steamin and he's been saying how hot Hogg looked all night. Then he just leaned in at the bar and kissed him! Look on Hoggs face was priceless!

21:59

JOHN:
*BIG bosses - not bif, lol!

22:00

SUZIE:
Is Hogg gay too?

22:00

JOHN:
Duncs not gay - just likes what he likes, men or women

22:02

SUZIE:
Sorry - but is the boss?

22:02
JOHN:
No, but he took it well! Laughed in the end

22:04
DD:
Why shouldn't he? I'm a catch!!

22:04
SUZIE:
WTF were you thinking, Dunc?

22:05
DD:
Wasn't! He was there, he was hot... lol

22:06
SUZIE:
He could have sacked you

22:08
DD:
Nah - sent me home maybe, but it was worth it

22:09
SUZIE:
Your mad!

22:09
SUZIE:
You're drunk!!

22:11
DD:
Not drunk enough! The nite is young...

Out Of India 14/12/24
to me

View this email in your browser

OUT OF INDIA

Your meal at Out Of India is booked

Date: Saturday 21st December
Time: 10.00pm
Covers: 2

We'll see you real soon!

If you need to cancel your reservation
Click here

22:15

X

H.A.G.(HotAsianGuy) @DrunkenDuncan • 4m

Heading into Merchant City for a curry and MORE BEER! Who wants to join me and JOhn? #OnTheTown #YOLO #MerchantCityBars #CurryFiend

💬 🔁 ♡ 📊 4 ↗

22:21

JEZ:
See ya at BrewDog at 11?

22:32

H:
Some of us have to work in the morning 😴

22:47

SUZIE:
How you going to get home?

23:12

JEZ:
I'm here!! Where R U?

23:15

DD:
On my way - Just paying for curry!!

23:55

SUZIE:
You still on your pub crawl?:

00:13

DD:
Yes just out Connollys

00:13

DD:
Looking fr taxi

00:18

DD:
ffs! 55 min wait!!

00:20

DD:
Might walk back:

00:21

DD:
Fuk its cold!

00:24

Duncan Chao 22/12/24
to Out Of India ⌄

HI there - i think I may have left my jacket with you! went back but you were shut. Black leather jkt, HUgo Boss but old. Pls could u keep it for me intil tomorroew. Thanx

Sun

-3°

Feels like -7°

Tap here for 24 hr forecast

04:15
DD: Suz - u there?

04:18
SUZIE: wtf Dunc??! I/m asleep

04:19
DD: Tried ringing. Hoped you had notifications on

04:19
SUZIE: Have u seen the time?? Fks sake

04:20
DD: I been robbed

04:21
DD: Can u come get me?

04:21
SUZIE: WHAT! Are u ok? Are u at the police station? Of course - I'll be there right away

04:22
DD: I'm not feeling good but ok. Not told cops, maybe tomorrow. I'm by the Clyde, can meet u at new McDs

04:22
DD: Don't tell anyone else

Journal
V2.23

Sun 22 Dec

Quote of the Day:
YOU ARE THE ARTIST OF YOUR OWN LIFE
Don't hand the paintbrush to someone else

Today's Entry:

God, my head hurts! And I feel like crap - must have caught a chill or something last night.

After party, went into town to carry on drinking with John. Somewhere along the way lost him - and my jacket! Bloody cold night too! No taxis so walked back along Clyde. Was very tired though and at some point stopped and sat on a bench. Woke up three hours later!! Could hardly move and my wallet was gone - think it was robbed while I slept. It was in my shirt pocket so pretty easy. Must contact police & cancel cards. Luckily phone was in my back pocket so they couldn't get to it! Don't know what I'd do if I lost this - my whole life is on here!!

Thanks to good old Suzie for picking me up - must get her chocolates or something. Still an expensive night out!! Fucking Christmas party!!

Today I'm feeling:

TO DO:
Never Drink Again!!

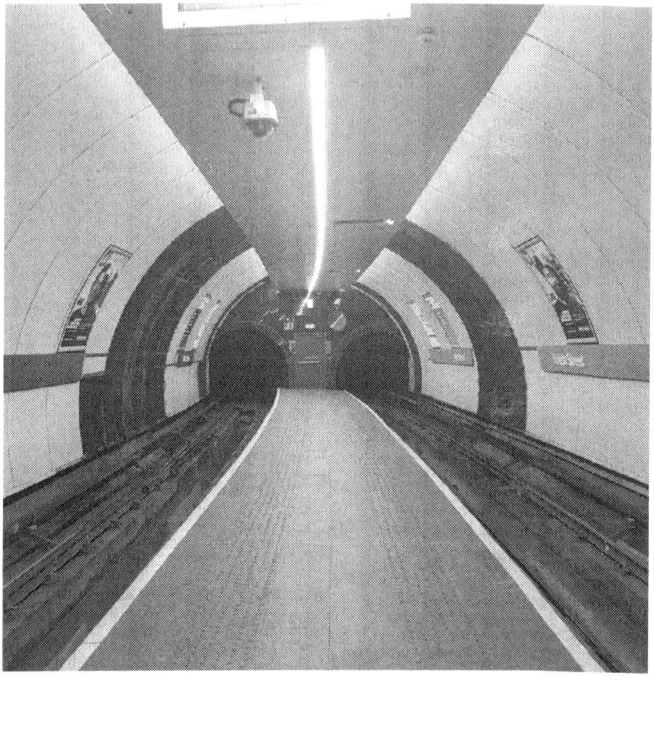

West Street

The concrete never warmed up. No matter what the time of year, no matter how hot the sun on him, the concrete beneath him stayed icily, bone-numbingly cold. Normally, he would put a piece of cardboard down first, insulation, but the night before some neds had found him and pissed all over him, laughing and threatening worse if he tried to run away, and the cardboard was useless now.

Garry woke to the sound of a car pulling up nearby. He hadn't really been asleep but it was the closest he got to it when on the streets. A sort of waking doze, one ear always alert for trouble. Cars were not trouble, usually, unless they were police cars and not always then, but they did signal the start of the day. With difficulty, he sat up, his aching body thankful for at least being under the shelter of the railway bridge.

Even so, he needed to be nearer to the subway station. People would be going to work from the nearby houses and flats, carrying coffees onto the escalators, bundled up against the cold. It was a good time to put the cup out. See if he could get any cash or maybe they would buy him breakfast. It happened occasionally.

Garry rolled up his fleeced blanket, filthy and stinking of someone else's piss, and tucked it away behind the rubbish bin by the bicycle racks. No one ever saw it there, not even the workers who came to empty the bin.

Then he stepped out in front of the Subway station and took his usual position just to the right of the entrance, cross-legged on the ground.

It wasn't a good morning. No one bought him breakfast. He recognised one of the women going into the Subway and hoped she might see him and help. She did see him, but immediately rushed past.

Then again, maybe it hadn't been her. Garry was finding it hard to concentrate, the lack of food and sleep making the world see-saw before him. His thoughts slipped away easily. He wasn't sure when he'd last eaten – possibly the previous morning. His stomach cramped at the memory.

One of the men passing him to get to the subway kicked his cup over.

"Hey!" Garry called out and the man looked back, surprised. Garry didn't think the surprise came from the challenge, more from the fact the man hadn't even seen him in the first place.

The man muttered something that might have been an apology, might have been a curse, and continued on his way. Garry picked up the cup. It was empty anyway. Since the pandemic, cash had become a rarity, with most people relying on card transactions. Which was no good to him.

Garry was exhausted. He didn't want to, but his head kept drooping, sleep taking over. He knew it was a bad thing – apart from leaving him vulnerable, most people saw a homeless man sleeping and thought them lazy. Especially if they were on the way to work themselves and had not long been torn from their own slumber. Sleep was a bad thing, but like so many bad things, it was oh so tempting.

A slight thud in front of him brought Garry to his senses. A coin had been dropped into his cup, two pounds. He looked up to see his benefactor.

The man was standing over him. He reached into his pocket and pulled out a fiver. The man glanced around quickly then crouched down to Garry's level.

"Here, get yourself some breakfast," he said.

Before Garry could thank him, the man continued.

"If you're here tonight, when I come home, you can come back to mine. Get a proper meal, a bath. Maybe a bed."

Garry looked at him. He knew what the man meant.

Taking the offered money, he nodded and the man winked back. "Good boy."

Garry would have loved a McDonald's burger but he couldn't go into any of the stores looking as he did. He knew from experience that he'd be thrown out as soon as he was spotted, whether he'd already ordered his food or not, and he couldn't risk losing his food.

Instead, he went a couple of streets over to a café. In reality, it was no more than a store front with a couple of tables and chairs outside, popular in the summer but not getting many takers at this time of year. Coffees and baked potatoes with a variety of fillings were sold from a serving hatch, cakes laid out behind the window beside it. It was popular with people heading into work, but more to the point, the owner didn't mind homeless people sitting and eating there as long as they could pay. It was a small thing but in Garry's world it carried great weight.

"What'll it be?" the woman behind the counter asked. She must have been in her forties and Garry didn't know if she was the owner or not, but she always seemed to be there.

"Jacket with baked beans," Garry said, choosing whatever he could think was the most filling. "Coffee. Lots of sugar." He handed over the five pound note and didn't get any change.

"Sugar's on the table, love. Be with you in a minute", the woman replied before dipping out of sight into the depths of the building.

Garry sat at the table furthest from the hatch, an unwritten rule in case any other customers came along and could be put off by his presence.

A few moments later and a hot cup of coffee (actually in a cup) and a baked potato completely buried under a mountain of baked beans appeared before him. The steam coming off the food in the cold morning air was warming enough in itself.

"I thought you might like one of these too," the woman said and produced an Eccles cake on a plate. "They were delivered yesterday, can't really sell them, but, well..."

Garry looked up at her and croaked a thank you. The steam, or something, was causing his eyes to water.

"Yeah, well, enjoy your food," the woman said and bustled off back to her counter.

It was unusual for Garry to get this little bit of kindness. Other guys he had met on the street seemed to think he might have a better chance of sympathy than them – only 23, blonde, good looking if you could see past the dirt – but it never seemed to work out that way.

Garry sat for a moment, enjoying the smell of the food before him, the warmth coming off it. He dearly wanted to dive straight into it, but he held back to savour the moment. He didn't want to feel as if he had lost all sense of civility despite his circumstances.

But he could feel his mouth watering at just the thought of food and so he picked up the knife and fork and started in on the plate. The first scoop of baked beans burnt his mouth slightly but the tang of the sauce, the richness of the taste, made it worth it. It was comforting, warming, and before he could stop it, the taste took him back to other times.

To a house and a family. A mother and a father and breakfasts that had included bacon, eggs, baked beans. Garry hated himself for remembering those days. Not just because they were gone but because of the other memories that always came with them. The arguments, the blows, being thrown out by his father. Sleeping on the couches of friends.

If he thought about it, but he rarely did, that would be where things really started to go wrong. His friends were wonderful at first, leaving him alone in their houses, telling him to help himself to whatever was in the fridge, but he started to feel isolated from them. He was living to their patterns. None of his belongings were around him, none of the decisions were his. He was powerless. He started taking long walks around the city centre, sitting in GOMA or the library for hours. Some nights he wouldn't return until he knew his friends had gone to bed, so that it might feel, briefly, as if he was stepping into a place of his own. It didn't work.

Then, one night, he just didn't go back. Strangely, it felt good, like he was making a decision for himself again. It was the end of summer and he slept in some bushes in Victoria Park. He'd arrived before the gates were locked and, hidden away, he felt unexpectedly secure. The next day, he decided to stay out again and somehow that became a week. He had money then, so it wasn't too bad. He could eat. He could use a gym for a shower. Gradually, however, the novelty wore off, the money ran out. His friends didn't seem to be looking for him and going back to them after such a break didn't seem like an option. He was completely alone.

In those early days, Garry had even tried a hostel. On his first night, somebody on another bunk pulled out some meth and a fight started over who should have it. Another man started shouting at the two fighters and Garry had never felt as close to terror as he did then. Even when his father had beaten him, it had been something he could predict, try to avoid. Here it was just sudden naked aggression, spontaneous and terrifying. Garry spent that night wide awake and never returned.

He picked up some sachets of sugar and added six of them to his coffee. The sugar rush would help him through the day, but the crash later would probably wipe him out. He wondered if the two pounds he had left would be enough to buy an energy drink.

Garry stuffed the Eccles cake into a pocket for later and finished the last of his hot food. He considered licking the plate clean of the tasty sauce but decided he had not yet fallen that far. That was the thing with being homeless – you could see where rock bottom was, could touch it, and it was your choice as to whether you took that step towards it or not. Little actions, taken or refused, could be enough to keep some self-esteem and Garry's life was filled with decisions sacrificed to keep him from the depths. Because the horror of it was, he knew that if he fell any further, he might not get back up.

After eating, Garry was feeling good enough to take the short walk into the city for the rest of the day. The area around West Street was busy first thing in the morning and later in the day, as people travelled to and from work, but for the rest of the day it was a concrete desert. If he wanted to try and get some more money, it would have to be away from the Subway station.

It was difficult in the centre, though. Lots of regulars had their own spots, carefully honed from months, sometimes years, of camping out in all weathers, all fiercely guarded. If he put his cup out too close to someone else's patch, Garry knew from bitter experience he could expect harsh words, an argument, even a fight. The only solution was to find a new spot and to hope that it was popular enough to get plenty of passers-by.

So far, he had not had much luck. He favoured a spot on the side of the Clyde, close to a building site. He liked to stay on the South side to be close to West Street. The footfall was quite good, and it wasn't an area that attracted the police very often, but the building site brought its own problems. Quite often, he would be moved on by burly construction workers, sent over by their managers who thought he was hanging around waiting for the chance to steal something.

There were other problems with the site too. Memories that he tried hard to push away.

Two months earlier, Garry had been at this position when a figure had stopped in front of him. As he had looked up to see who it was, something wet hit him in the face. Garry wiped the spittle from his cheek and squinted into the sun.

"Shoulda fuckin' known you'd end up like this," a voice said. "Useless cunt."

Garry knew the harsh tone to the voice and instinctively cowered at the familiar sound. The arm that had wiped his cheek had stayed up, defensively.

"You're not worth the effort," his father had said and turned away.

Garry had watched him walk off down the path with a mixed sense of relief and loneliness. He had never seriously expected to go home, but that didn't mean he hadn't fantasised about it. Warmth, comfort, a loving family, they had all felt as if they were still, somehow, within reach. Now he couldn't even pretend it might come true.

That night Garry had done something he rarely did – he spent his money on Buckfast and passed out under the railway bridge, hot tears soaking into the uncaring pavement, no longer bothering if anyone found him or not.

He hadn't seen his father since that day. Whether it had been an aberration for him to walk that way or if he now took a different route to avoid his son didn't matter. That pathway was closed to him.

There was rain in the air as the commuters started to return home.

Garry was there to meet them, a new piece of cardboard underneath him, filched from a skip behind the building site.

Part of him was keeping an eye out for the man who had spoken to him that morning. Garry hadn't decided yet if he would go with him. It wasn't the first time he'd been approached and, given his youth and looks, it wasn't unexpected. The surprise had been that it wasn't always by men.

The first time had been with a woman. She'd been a kindly looking older woman, matronly even. One dark and cold night, she had invited him back to her flat for some food and Garry, new to the streets, took her at face value.

Once they had got there, she had also volunteered to wash his clothes. His request for a towel was swiftly denied.

"No," the woman had said. "I want to see you."

The weather outside had gotten worse, but Garry considered leaving at that point, food or not.

"I won't touch you," the woman had said. "You're quite safe. But I want to look."

So, he had stayed, and true to her word, the woman never touched him. She watched him shower and towel himself dry (asking for the towel back straight after) and then she cooked him a meal while he sat, naked, at her kitchen table. After that, she watched him eat and they talked about the weather and Glasgow and favourite foods, anything that wouldn't draw attention to his own situation or the strange ritual that was taking place in her mind. Every now and then, Garry would see her looking at his crotch, but it seemed more out of curiosity than lust.

Then, just as he had settled into the weirdness of the situation, she had presented him with his freshly laundered and dried clothes and told him to get out. He never saw her again.

Not everyone was as safe, however. The first man he had been with, who had also offered a shower and food, had tried to suck his cock when they got back to his small apartment. When Garry had refused, he turned violent and Garry only just got out without a beating, the man yelling at him as he ran, stumbled, fell down the stairs. After that, Garry took to carrying a knife around, small and stolen from that same man's kitchen, keeping it sharp by rubbing it on curb stones on lonely nights. He had been with other men since, even though that was not his thing by choice. On the whole, they were kinder than the first one, wanting mainly to service him, and for a brief moment, with his eyes shut, it made him feel good to be wanted.

There were a couple of coins in his cup by the time the man appeared, one of the last commuters of the day. He stood in front of Garry, looking around before saying, "Hello again."

Garry looked up. The man had kindly eyes. His build was not unlike Garry's father's.

"Hi," Garry replied.

"Have you thought about my offer?" the man said. "Would you like to come home with me?"

"I get a meal and a bath?" Garry said.

The man nodded. His voice dropped slightly, even though no one else was around.

"If you'll let me, I'll even wash you myself. Then maybe, later, I can help you relax as well."

"And a bed for the night?" Garry asked.

"We'll see how it goes," the man replied.

"Okay," said Garry. "But one thing more. I want you to hold me. Hug me. Doesn't have to be for long. Do you think you can do that?"

The man looked at him strangely for a moment, then nodded. "After," he said.

Garry stood up and folded his piece of cardboard. He took it over to the bin and tucked it behind his blanket, then came back over to the man. Stood beside him, Garry could see that he was the same height as his father too.

"Let's go," he said. He reached out and touched the man's arm briefly.

His other hand stayed in his pocket, around the comforting sharpness of the knife.

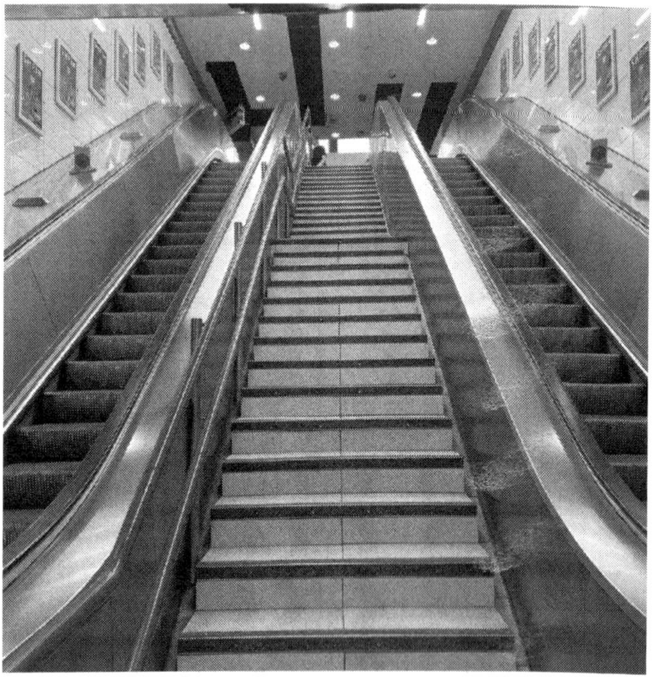

Govan to **Bridge Street** to St Enoch

Marie had wanted to see the Govan Stones for some time but getting to them had not been easy. First, she had needed someone to drive her from her home in Cambuslang to Govan. Luckily, her neighbour, Sylvie, had been coming into town anyway and didn't mind the slight detour. They had managed to find accessible parking in nearby Pearce Street, but Sylvie had been quite bothered about leaving her friend on her own. Marie calmed her.

"I've been navigating the streets with this chair for over fifteen years," she said. "I think I've got the hang of it by now."

As if to prove this, the pavements of Govan proved surprisingly even and the short trip to Govan Old Church gave the wheelchair no problems at all. From there, however, things got tougher. The pathway up to the church doors was made from old flagstones and brick and meandered through the old graveyard in a much less favourable way. There were odd moments when her chair lurched slightly as a wheel caught the side of an uneven paving stone, and by the time Marie had reached the doors of the church she was sweating slightly in the summer sun.

A set of steps had faced her, but she had been prepared for this. She did not have long to wait until a short, bearded man popped out of the building, saw her, said hello and then nipped back inside again. He and another man then re-emerged with a large metal ramp.

"Glad you rang ahead," the man said as the two of them wrangled the huge object into place. "It takes some time to get this set up."

It had, indeed, been a chore, leaving Marie to wonder why they hadn't set the thing up in advance. It didn't inconvenience other visitors, so why not prepare for her arrival? But in the end, it was done and she was able to enter the cool shadows of the church to finally see the stones.

The Govan Stones. She had read about them and seen photos of them, but nothing prepared her for the physicality of actually being amongst them. Scattered throughout the now defunct church, the stones were carved relics of a time before even this ancient building had existed. Marie marvelled at their size. There were five Viking hogback stones that particularly took her attention. Huge sandstone blocks, carved into arched shapes with intricate patterning across their bodies. The information card beside them suggested that they were designed to resemble Scandinavian longhouses, but to Marie the shape was more like a great creature, curled up and at rest, the repeated patterns on their backs reminiscent of a lizard's scales.

Sleeping dragons, she thought.

Unfortunately, there was not enough room for Marie to manoeuvre her chair between the stones, so she was unable to examine anything beyond the ones closest to the pathway. Elsewhere, carved crosses and cross shafts were accessible to her, and each was fascinating in their own way, but, before she left, Marie found herself drawn back to the hogbacks.

Her hand caressed the stone, tracing the carved lines within it, feeling how it had been worn down by age and the touch of thousands, maybe millions, of other people through the ages. She closed her eyes briefly and thought of all those souls, all the fleeting touches, lost to time while the stone endured - cold, unfeeling, yet comforting in its permanence.

For a moment, she allowed herself a flight of fantasy, imagining that her touch awakened something in the stone, a great beast unfurling before her, wings opening to be caressed by the air in a way they had not felt in centuries. In her mind, the beast bowed its head to her and, daintily, she stepped out of the chair and rode on its back instead, leaving the church and its awkward ramps far, far behind.

She stayed like that, one hand on the stone, her thoughts far away, eyes closed but open to the sunlight of an imagined world, until the fantasy could not sustain itself any longer and she had to return to the dim interior of the church.

There was another reason for coming to Govan, and that was because it was one of only two Subway stations that had a lift and it was therefore accessible to a wheelchair user. Marie wanted to get into town, and she was curious to see the Subway system in action.

Her first problem, however, became evident as she approached the ticket office. It was a large, mostly glass booth, with a ticketing window raised high off the ground. Marie pulled up in front of the desk but soon realised that she was below the level of the ticket officer's eyeline. She pulled back a bit to be seen. This in turn meant that, when the ticket officer did notice her, they virtually had to shout at one another to be heard.

"I'd like a ticket to St Enoch's, please."

The ticket seller, a stocky man with thick white hair, stood up from his seat to better see her.

"Hello," he said, then after a pause: "Did you ring ahead?"

Marie shook her head. She knew that, when travelling by train, it was advised that patrons with access needs rang ahead by at least three hours to give the station warning, but she had never agreed with the policy. So, all disabled people had to know their timetables well in advance? Where was the spontaneity? Where was the adventure? Yes, the station staff needed to get a ramp out on the platform for anyone in a chair, but it wasn't like they had to bring them very far and Marie always arrived in good time for any train she wanted. Besides, this was the Subway –

she'd checked the website and there was no such provision here.

Even so, the ticket officer looked a little put out by her negative response. "Just a minute," he said.

Marie watched as he quickly looked around the ticket office for another person, but it remained resolutely empty. Eventually, he picked up a radio and made a call to someone elsewhere. The ticket officer turned away from the window when a reply came through, but Marie could see from his body language that a slightly heated conversation was taking place. After a few moments, the ticket officer turned back to Marie with a slightly pained smile.

"Someone will be with you in just a moment," he said.

Marie looked around the very empty station foyer but nevertheless smiled and pulled back from the ticket office. A couple of minutes later, a young man appeared. His hair was starting to thin and he was a lot skinnier than his colleague in the booth, but his smile seemed genuine.

"Hi there," he said, extending a hand. "Ah'm Anthony. How kin I help you the noo?"

Marie shook the proffered hand with an amused look and repeated that she would like to buy a ticket for St Enoch's. Anthony asked if she had a payment card and when the answer was yes, directed her across to the ticket machines by the entrance. He stayed with her, just to make sure everything was okay, but didn't try to interfere or offer advice. Marie decided that she quite liked him.

Ticket bought, she turned back to him and declared, "Lead on, good Sir Anthony!"

The young man blushed slightly – in quite a fetching manner, Marie thought – and gestured over to the opposite side of the foyer. There she could see the twin silver doors of a lift.

While they waited for the lift to arrive, Anthony started up a small conversation.

"Hae ye travelled by the Subway afore?" he asked.

Marie shook her head. "No, it's all a big adventure," she said. "I'm going into town to see an opera at the Theatre Royal."

"Oh," Anthony replied, and she realised that he was probably making small adjustments to the way he thought of her. It was funny – dropping the O word into conversation often led people to make more assumptions about her than seeing the chair did. Opera was elitist or boring or just something far out of the listener's comfort zone. It was a rare occasion when it did not provoke a response.

"I've no, er, no been," Anthony said, and as he did the doors to the lift slid silently open. Marie was pleased to see that it was a good-sized compartment, with room for her to go in and turn around without too much trouble. She moved forward.

"You should try it," she said as she went past him. "It can be very entertaining. It's not all fat women in Viking helmets."

Anthony smiled and joined her in the lift. "Och, I ken that. There's like... *Carmen*, is it? And that wan set in Egypt what Elton John deed the music far."

It was Marie's turn to smile. "Well, I think Verdi beat him to it, if you mean *Aida* – but yes, there's a variety of things you can see, funny and serious."

There was a pause as the lift descended. "In fact, the opera I'm going to tonight is by Verdi as well. *Rigoletto*."

"Aye, I think I've heard of that wan," Anthony said. "Dinna know what it's about, though."

Marie was just about to give him a quick version of the story when the lift doors opened and she got her first glance at the white-tiled hall that housed the platforms. Marie knew that some stations had a central platform, but Govan was one of those with two separate sides. She looked out of the doors and could see, on the other side of the rails, the mirror of her own platform.

She exited the lift and stopped just outside it. "Oh my!" she said.

Anthony had followed her out. "Whit is it?" he asked, his face a picture of concern.

"I just hadn't expected something so big," Marie said, looking around. The platform stretched away beyond her, posters lining the walls on both sides, pristine white edged along the top with an orange flash. She moved forwards to see the trough that the rail lines lay in.

"Yeah, I suppose we get used to – hey, now, watch yersel!" Anthony said. He glanced up at the information board. "Yer train will be here in wan minute. Don't get too close."

Marie moved back a bit, noting that there were also raised bobbles, like the underside of Lego tiles, before she got to the edge.

"So, the best steid for ye tae get oan is ower here," Anthony was saying. "There's nae ramp, I'm afraid, but the train is pretty level with the flair. There's a bit of a gap, but it shouldnae be so wide ower here."

Marie followed his lead and moved over to the far left of the platform.

"Er, normally we ask wheelchair passengers to get oot o' the chair n' fold it up," Anthony said. His face had gone red again. "But then usually, the passenger is travelling wi' someone and..."

He glanced down to Marie's legs and the binding that went across them, securing her to the chair. It was a very quick look, but she noticed it still.

"I'll not be getting out," she said. "And, as you can see, there's no one travelling with me. Unless you want to accompany me."

Anthony went a shade redder. "I... I'm nae..." he started, but Marie took pity on him.

"I'm just pulling your leg," she said. "I'll manage fine on my own."

A gust of cold wind blew her hair into her eyes briefly and then suddenly there was a roaring noise approaching them. As Marie looked round, a phrase from earlier jumped into her mind. *Sleeping dragons*, but sleeping no more, she thought. With a squeal of brakes, the train emerged from the tunnel and snaked its way towards her.

The doors were only a short distance away from where Anthony had suggested, and there were a few people to get off first. She noticed Anthony wave to the driver briefly, and then he turned to her and said, "Nae rush".

Marie moved forward. The gap between train and platform was slightly bigger than she'd expected and she wondered if her two smaller front wheels would cross it safely.

"Dae ye mind if I help?" Anthony asked, seeing her hesitation.

Marie hated needing help, but she also recognised when it was necessary. She gave Anthony a curt nod and he helped to push her into the carriage.

Once there, she could see that there was a couple of small seats, empty and facing one another, to her left, Marie turned her chair so that she could back into the space between them. It was snug, but it meant that she wasn't blocking the door. She put her brakes on and looked up at her assistant.

"I'll let them ken ye're oan yer way to St Enochs," he said, "and someone will catch up wi' ye there."

"Thank you. You've been a great help," Marie said, and she meant it.

"Enjoy your *Cannelloni*," Anthony replied. She was just about to correct him when she saw the grin on his face. Anthony winked at her and then jumped off the train. She saw him wave to the driver and then the doors closed behind him.

There were six stops between Govan and St Enoch's. Marie spent them watching the other people getting on and off the train and marvelling at how noisy the experience was. It was something she had never considered, that the distance between each station would be filled with the harsh sound of the wheels on the tracks, of the dragon roaring its way through the darkness.

By the time she reached Bridge Street, just one stop away from her destination, Marie was ready to get off. The train was also quite busy at that point and a lot of people were standing up. Every now and then, someone would shoot her a black look because her chair was taking up the space between available seats, but Marie ignored them. It was no longer surprising how people were sympathetic towards her up until the point her disability inconvenienced them.

The train pulled into Bridge Street and a few people got off. Hardly anyone was there to get on. Still, however, the doors did not close. Marie could see a few passengers looking at each other as the minutes dragged on.

Then a harsh metallic voice cut through the cabin. "Due to a defect, this train has now terminated passenger service," it said. The message repeated once more. There were no more instructions, but everyone else in the compartment seemed to know what it meant. With a look of determined certainty, they started to get off the train.

Marie felt a slight flutter of panic. She didn't know this station, had only a vague notion of where it was in the city, but she knew one thing about it: it didn't have a lift. If she was stuck here, there was no getting out without the humiliation of being carried out.

The compartment was almost empty now. First things first, she thought. You need to get off this train.

One of the other passengers, a young woman, had stopped and was now looking at her.

"I'm sorry," she said. "Please don't take offence, but do you, do you need a hand?"

Marie was about to say no and then thought better of it. "I might need a slight push to get over the gap," she said. "If you don't mind."

The woman nodded and waited for Marie to move forward. The gap between train and platform was slightly bigger here than it had been in Govan and she knew that her wheels wouldn't clear it easily. As she approached it, she asked the woman to give her a strong push. Marie felt the front wheels dip into the space and, for just a moment, she feared that the whole chair would up-end, but then she was over the gap and her back wheels were coping with it as if there had been no problem.

Marie thanked the young woman and then watched as she vanished up some stairs to, presumably, the outside world.

She now had the opportunity to look around at her new surroundings. Quite a few of the other passengers had decided to leave as well, but there were still around 30 or so people on the platform. Unlike Govan, this was a station with a central platform, trains for the Inner circle approached on one side of her and for the Outer on the other. Marie could see a slight curve as the tiled flooring stretched out before her. At her end of it, there were stairs; at the far end, it was a wall flanked by the twin tunnels. Neither was of any use to her.

Marie considered her options. There had been no announcements saying that all trains had been cancelled (although, for that matter, there had been no announcements about anything), so she had to assume that things were still working. She had travelled this far on the Inner Circle, so she could get on a train on the Outer Circle line and either return to Govan or travel round the complete loop until she reached St Enoch's that way. The information board was saying that the next Outer Circle train arrived in two minutes.

As she thought about her options, the train she had come in on closed its doors and pulled away from the station, heading in the direction she wanted to go. Marie couldn't see what the fault was, but also conceded that she wasn't a transport engineer either. She just hoped that there was some form of siding in the tunnels ahead of it so the line would not be blocked for any longer. Travelling one more stop to her destination was infinitely preferable to travelling thirteen.

She felt a rush of air again and realised that the Outer Line train was arriving. She spun her chair around to face it, but was immediately dismayed. It was full. Even before it had stopped, Marie could see people pressed up against the doors. Sure enough, when the train pulled up and the doors opened, very few people got off, and those that did had to push their way forwards to escape. There was no way Marie was going to be able to find a space for her chair.

Marie put her brakes on and allowed the exiting passengers to flow around her to the stairs. She felt briefly like a rock in a stream, water rushing around it whilst the stone was incapable of moving anywhere.

When the train pulled away, there were only three other people left on the platform and they were much further along the walkway.

Marie sighed. She didn't often let things get to her. The chair to her was a means to an end; at worst an inconvenience, at best a challenge. It had taken her a few years to come to this realisation – that she wasn't the chair, that it didn't define her – but there were times when all the imagination in the world couldn't overcome the annoyance of it. The inconvenience. Sometimes the world just didn't seem to want her there.

Something flickered in the corner of her eye and she saw the information board change. The next train on the Inner Line was now due in 6 minutes. The next Outer train was due before that, but Marie decided it was worth waiting it out to see if she could get this new train instead.

It was a long wait and she felt the solitude of being on the platform acutely. The Outer train came and went. Its carriages were almost empty, as if the universe wanted to test her resolve, to mock her stoicism.

To take her mind off her situation, Marie focussed on the evening ahead. She was looking forward to seeing *Rigoletto* – it had been the first opera she had ever seen and as such remained a favourite. At the time, though, she had not been interested in going. A friend dragged her along as a way of getting her out of herself after the accident. Marie had doubted that a tale of revenge, moral corruption and curses would lift her spirits, but she had allowed herself to be taken anyway.

In the end, it was transformative. The set had been huge, far beyond what she had expected, and expert lighting and design moved it from a Duke's court to a humble hovel with ease and skill. The story had been engrossing, with unexpected twists and a feeling that fate was waiting around every corner. It had been far more than the 'Shakespeare with music' that she had expected. And, oh, that music! Marie had been hooked from the moment the title character began to sing, his deep baritone voice not just impressive but an actual presence in the room. She had felt his words resounding in her chest, taking on the emotions of his journey despite it being sung in a language she didn't understand. The rest of the cast were superb as well, but in the end it was the jester, the cripple, the hunchback walking painfully at times on two sticks, who spoke to her.

Marie knew that nothing could ever recapture the magic of that night, of the discovery she had made, but subsequent trips to the Opera had yielded new delights for her. Comic opera became a particular favourite of hers, with a recent production of *The Barber of Seville* having made her laugh throughout. But no matter what the subject matter, it was the singing that mattered. It had the power to transport her beyond her life as it was.

As the Inner train pulled in, Marie realised she was humming *La donna e mobile* from that evening's score. It made her smile.

The doors slid open and she realised that no one was standing in front of them. There was room for her to get on, even to turn around if need be. With a determined push, Marie forced her chair over the slight gap and into the waiting space. The feeling of relief was incredible.

She trusted that Anthony would have rung ahead and there would be someone waiting for her at the next station. From there, it would be a coffee in the shopping centre and then making her way to the Theatre Royal for later. Things were back on track.

"Onwards," Marie said as the doors closed in front of her, and the dragon roared into the tunnel once more. "Ever onwards."

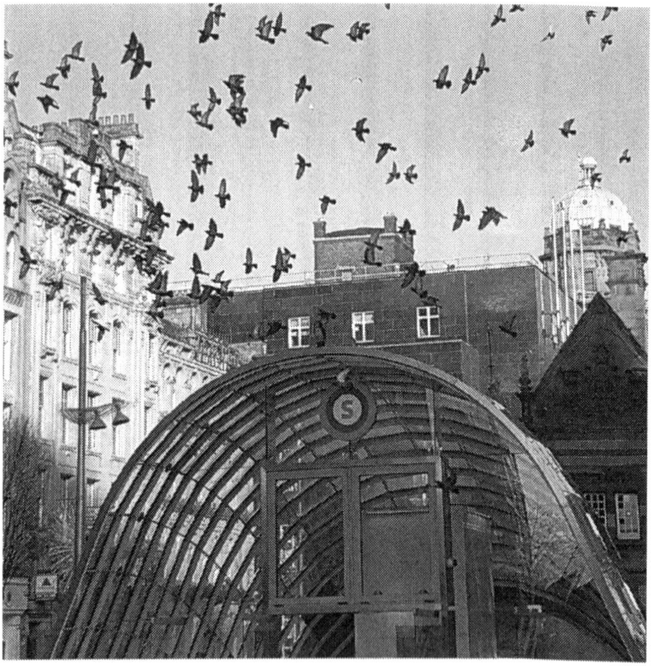

St Enoch

As she emerged into the sunshine from the depths of the Subway, Alice paused for a moment to take in her surroundings. It had been a long time since she had been to Glasgow and a lot had changed.

The last time had been in 1975, when she was in her early thirties. At the time, she'd thought it was the end of Glasgow. Back then, the grand St Enoch Hotel had stood derelict for almost a year, its dark mass looming over the long-abandoned railway station. Alice could remember looking around the area, the iron skeleton of the station building being used as a car park, the stones of the hotel and the shops around it painted black with soot and grime from the once busy railway. Beeching and his cuts were held to blame, stripping the railway stations in the city from four to just two, but that had been in 1966 and nothing had come to replace the grandeur of the station since. Alice couldn't help wondering if Glasgow was just giving up.

Two years later, the hotel and the station were demolished and work began on the St Enoch's shopping centre. But Alice hadn't been there. She'd moved away to Inverness with work and never had the desire to come back.

The St Enoch centre was bigger than the Hotel had been but she didn't feel it's presence as much. Perhaps it was the light stone and the glass that did it, reflecting back the sunny day rather than absorbing it the way the Hotel had. Perhaps it was because she wasn't connected to it, had never been inside the new building. Or perhaps it was because she had read that it too was destined for demolition, making it just a transitory thing, the past vanishing around her.

She came out of the cover of the glass subway arch and turned to her right. As she did, her breath caught in her throat. Before her was the old St Enoch's Subway entrance, a bizarrely beautiful and romantic building, perfect and yet adrift amongst all the new sights. Alice had always thought that it looked like the top of a tower, its turrets and wildly detailed stonework almost too much for a mere two storey building. To see it again was a shock as well as a welcome surprise.

As she looked at it, Alice could see differences between the building she had known and the one now before her. Most obviously, the grand gold letters that had sat beneath its clock, proudly proclaiming 'Underground', were gone, replaced by the name of the coffee shop the building now housed. The turrets were pristine rather than having the words 'St Enoch' written down them in smaller letters. The stone was freshly scrubbed so that its true red showed through. It was the same building and yet it wasn't.

There were tables set out in front of it, some with pale blue umbrellas to help against the summer sun. A few people were scattered around, drinking coffee, and one, sat on her own, no drink in front of her, was waving to Alice.

"I'm so glad you came," the woman said as Alice approached. She stood up, with a little difficulty, and hugged the newcomer. Alice was surprised by the action – she didn't remember Margaret as being physical, but it had been a long time since she had seen her. People changed.

"What would you like to drink?" Margaret said. "I'll nip in and get us something."

"Just a coffee," Alice said.

"Latte? Americano? Do you have milk? I only have soy milk now – my tummy can't take real milk the way it used to. I think they do coconut milk too. It's amazing what you can get these days."

"Just a straightforward coffee will do," said Alice. She had never got the hang of all the different types of coffee there seemed to be now.

"Okay," said Margaret. "You watch the table and I'll be back in a minute."

Left on her own again, Alice sat at the table and looked out at an unidentifiable St Enoch Square, wondering, not for the first time that day, why she was there.

She hadn't seen Margaret in nearly 50 years. The white-haired woman who had greeted her was clearly still the same young woman she had worked with on the St Enoch station ticketing counters – the mannerisms, the eagerness to please, the chattiness, all of that came flooding back as soon as Alice saw her. The eyes were the same too. Surrounded by wrinkles and hiding behind glasses now, but still unmistakably her.

Yet, until a few months ago, the two hadn't spoken in decades.

Margaret had contacted her on Facebook, curious to see if this Alice Shepherd was the same one she had worked with all those years ago. They had chatted on and off, remembering the glory days of St Enoch station, the camaraderie of the past. It was pleasant but Alice had initially been wary of renewing the contact. She was in Aberdeen now, retired, alone, and this bright chatty woman with her pictures of her grandchildren and posts of her son and daughter's successes was a little too much for her.

Not that Alice was unhappy – she had chosen a single life. She had friends; men friends too who were perhaps something more than that, even at her age. But a family, a life with someone, that had passed her by. Only once had she considered it, but that had been in another time, another place.

With a clatter, Margaret returned and put a tray down on the table.

"I got us some shortbread too," she said. "They have a huge choice of things in there, all sorts of cakes and pastries, but I didn't know what you liked, and I thought, well, everybody likes shortbread, so..."

Alice took the proffered shortbread on a plate and the coffee that came with it, thanking Margaret as she did.

The two of them sat next to one another, looking out at the square.

"It's good of you to come all this way," Margaret said. "Is your hotel alright?"

Alice assured her that it was and that the journey was no problem. "I should get out more anyway," she said. "And I haven't seen Glasgow in years."

"I bet it's changed a lot," Margaret said.

"Well, not this bit," Alice said, gesturing up at the front of the coffee shop.

"Yes," Margaret said. "I remember you used to like this building. Jim used to say it reminded him of the top of a tower."

Alice looked up at her, briefly startled at the comparison with her own thoughts.

"I... I was sorry to hear that he had passed," she said.

Margaret looked down at her coffee and took a moment before replying. "Thank you," she said. "Forty two years together. Well, married. We were courting for about two years before that. I still miss him."

They were both quiet for a moment. Then Margaret said, "It was six years ago, though. You move on. Literally, in my case. I moved house 18 months ago. That place was far too big for me. Got a nice little ground floor tenement flat now. Much better."

Alice smiled and drank some coffee. As Margaret continued on about her new flat, she thought about one of the last times she had seen Jim.

He and Margaret had just announced their engagement. There wasn't a party or anything, no one could afford that, just a few drinks down the pub. He was as pleased as she'd ever seen him. His dark hair had been brylcreemed into place, brown eyes twinkling as he pulled Margaret in towards him. The room had been full of cigarette smoke and promise.

"Listen to me prattle on," Margaret cut into her thoughts. "What about you? How are you these days?"

Alice reflected a moment at the way the question was phrased, as if it had only been a few weeks since they'd seen each other, not half a lifetime. "Oh, I'm fine," she said.

She told Margaret about how she had moved around Scotland for work, about her life now in Aberdeen, how she had a good pension from the PA position she had ended up in for the last twenty years of her working life, how she owned her own flat. All things to do with her surface life.

Margaret nodded along as Alice spoke, interjecting the odd time to say how wonderful something was or to ask for some curious detail. At first, Alice found it a little annoying but as the conversation flowed, she realised this was how they had always been, back in the day, and it was nice to fall into the rhythm again, comforting. A friendship rediscovered.

"Do you ever hear from any of the others from the station?" Alice asked.

Margaret thought for a moment. "Well, unfortunately most of them are dead," she said and gave a little guilty laugh. "I mean, it's sad, but it's true. There's no point pretending we're not at that age, is there?"

Alice nodded. She'd forgotten that Margaret could be fairly blunt if she wanted to be.

"But Charlie's still around," she said. "You remember Charlie? Big guy, mutton chop beard, supposedly he was a ticket collector but mostly he was kept around to frighten any young neds who were messing about."

"Oh, god – Charlie!" Alice said, laughing herself. "I'd forgotten about him. I'm surprised he's still going –

he smoked two packs of Capstan a day, didn't he? Remember that time he chased those kids across all twelve platforms? God, I thought he'd have a heart attack there and then!"

"He still caught the little buggers, though, didn't he?"

Alice laughed. "And booted them out!"

The two of them smiled at the memory. Alice felt some of the tension in her shoulders ease up.

"Did you ever go in the hotel?" Margaret asked.

Alice smiled at her, wondering where the question had come from. "No, I don't think so," she said. "Don't remember it. Did you?"

"No, never lucky enough," Margaret smiled. "Always wanted to. There was a sort of grandeur to it. It was special. First place in Glasgow to get electric lighting, did you know that?"

"Course I did!" Alice said. "But it wasn't special for that. The station got it at the same time. It was a job lot."

Margaret nodded. "Yeah, but the hotel was different. It was magical. Jim went there once, he said. But not with me." She paused. "Do you fancy another drink?"

Alice looked down at her empty cup. "My turn. What are you having? And soy milk, wasn't it?"

Margaret nodded and told her exactly what to order. Alice got up and went into the coffee shop, slowly repeating the order in her mind so as to get it right.

The inside of the shop was nothing like the building she remembered. There was no trace of the subway station it had once been and Alice was quite sad to realise it. She ordered her drinks and was pleased when they didn't take long to make. Picking up some more shortbread, she took the drinks outside.

Margaret was sat at the table, but now she had a small book in front of her. There was a rubber band across the middle of it and Alice could see other papers wedged between the pages. Alice put the tray down without saying anything.

"Thanks," Margaret said. "They make a nice coffee here, don't they?"

Alice nodded and was just about to say something else, something innocuous, when Margaret said, "It's funny what you find when you move house."

"Sorry?" Alice said, but her eyes went to the book on the table.

"I mean, moving from my big place, a family home, to a flat – I mean, a fairly big flat, but still – moving from one to the other, you have to do some downsizing."

"I would imagine so," Alice said, but Margaret carried on as if she hadn't heard her.

"So, I ended up going through all sorts of things that I'd previously put aside. Things from when Jim died. I mean, as I say, six years. At first, it's because you don't want to touch them, because they're private things and you feel wrong looking at them. If he didn't show them me when he was alive, you think, he wouldn't want me looking at them now he's not around. And time goes past and you sort of forget about them. Not completely, not wholly. There's always a bit of you wondering what that part of him was that he didn't want to share, but you don't want to pry. You don't want to hurt yourself."

Margaret stopped for a second and took a sip of her coffee.

"Ooh, that's nice," she said. "Thanks for that. Anyway, then I came to move and there they were again. Just a shoebox really, with some photos and a book. And I had to decide, do I look or do I throw it all away? Do I want to know?"

Her finger was idly stroking the book. Alice didn't think she was even aware she was doing it.

"So, you looked?" Alice said.

"Yes, dear," Margaret said. Her tone had changed. She was more resigned about something now. "The photos, well, they were nothing. Pictures of his Mum and Dad, him as a kid, holiday photos. I don't know why he kept them hidden really. The book, however." She paused, then carried on. "I never knew he kept a diary. I mean, he didn't after we got married. I suppose only the young have time for things like that. Once you get married, you're too busy and by the time you get to our age, well, there's nothing worth putting in one, is there?"

She smiled at Alice. The tension was back in Alice's shoulders and she made a conscious effort to relax them.

"Margaret," she said.

"So, anyway, he had this diary," Margaret tapped the book with one finger. "Full of all his old escapades. Before he knew me. After. Almost right the way up to our wedding day."

"It was nothing, Margaret. Just youth," Alice said.

"Oh, I know that," Margaret said. Alice noticed that the other woman was unable to meet her eyes. "I don't blame you. He was a handsome devil, my Jim. And by all accounts, you were there first. I mean, you are part of the diary before I am. But then we meet and we go courting and he's still seeing you. Still meeting you under the clock at the station."

"He chose you," Alice said.

"Did he?" Margaret asked. "I know he ended up with me. But you were the one he took to the Hotel, two days after our engagement party. You were the one he writes about the most. There must have been something between you two or you would have just given up. You wouldn't have lied to me today about the hotel."

The two women sat in silence for a moment. Margaret lifted her drink to her lips, her hand shaking slightly.

"What is it you want?" Alice said. "Why did you want to see me again?"

A young girl, no more than 5 or 6 years old, suddenly ran up to the table, all giggles and noisy chaos. Alice should have been annoyed at the interruption, but instead it seemed to break a spell. It was faintly bizarre that they were sat outside, in a public square, in a coffee shop, having this conversation after so many years. She supposed it had always been there, waiting for her somewhere in her future, but she would not have expected it here, now. As the young girl's mother pulled her away with muttered apologies, Alice looked down at the book on the table.

"Those papers sticking out of the diary - are they my letters?" she said.

Margaret nodded.

"Then if he saved all of them," Alice said, "you'll see that I didn't want to break up. It was his doing. The last letter I wrote to him pleaded for him to leave you. To run away with me. But he wouldn't. He loved you, Margaret. That night in the hotel, that was our last night together. That's why he took me there – to say goodbye."

Margaret looked up, took her hand off the book for the first time.

"He did choose you," Alice said.

"Thank you," Margaret said, finally looking up to see her again. "I just... just needed to know that. Ever since I read the diary, I've been thinking back. To times when he just didn't seem to be there, when I'd catch him lost in a world of his own. And at the time, I thought he was just daydreaming, just taking a break, but since the diary... well, I look back and wonder if he had regrets. If there was a path he felt he should have taken."

"They were just daydreams," Alice said. "Probably thinking about fishing or something. I doubt he ever gave me another thought."

Margaret nodded. She brushed a tear away and visibly pulled herself together.

"You'll understand if I leave now," she said. "I need to be on my own."

Alice nodded and watched as she put the book away in her bag. Suddenly, Alice wanted to hug her again, but she knew she couldn't. Instead, she reached across the table and took the other woman's hand, held it briefly, silently.

"Thank you," Margaret said again as she started to leave. "You know, that last letter isn't in there." She tapped the side of her bag absentmindedly. "Jim must have destroyed it. I'm glad you told me about it. That was very brave of you."

Alice watched her as Margaret walked off across the square, heading for the Subway station.

A cloud passed over the sun and just for a moment Alice was transported back to the days of the St Enoch hotel towering over the square, casting its own shadow over everything and everyone.

It had been an easy lie. One that a friend tells to save further heartache.

There had been no final letter, not like that anyway. Jim had taken her to the hotel that night and, in bed, entwined, had told her he thought he'd made a mistake getting engaged. That he didn't know if he was ready. And Alice, who really did want to keep him, who really had seen a life together for both of them, realised that Jim probably never would be satisfied, probably never could settle down without wondering what he had missed out on. With Margaret or with her, there would always be the regret of what could have been.

So, Alice broke up with him, that night, in that room, overlooking the train station and the entrance to the Subway. She made the decision that would shape her life, and that of Margaret, forever. She didn't regret it, but it stayed with her for the rest of her life. It was an echo that she took into every relationship from then on.

The sun came out again and Alice finished her coffee. She looked around the square, thinking how much it had changed, how she had been wrong about

Glasgow giving up all those years ago. For a moment, she wondered if she had been the one giving up instead. She had thought she was striking out alone, but could she have been running away?

Alice shook her head and stood up. There was no point in following that path. The past was done and, like the square around her, things changed. Aberdeen awaited her, and she left the square with a renewed resolution to make new memories.

Biographies

Steven Blockley was born in Scotland and, after living a life of travel, returned to make it his home once more. A proud Glaswegian, his Italian and Greek heritage and the exploits of his Great Grandfather, Jack Lemm, helped form the basis of his first book, *The Welsh Hercules*.

David J Thacker originally hailed from North West England but made Glasgow his home a few years ago, thereby fulfilling a lifelong dream of moving to Scotland. He is a theatre professional and has also written several other books (all available from Amazon)

**If you enjoyed this book,
why not try our novel based on
the true story of Jack Lemm,
fairground strongman**

**JACK LEMM·
The WELSH
HERCULES!**

Snapshots of a
Strongman's Life

S Blockley
&
D J Thacker

**"An entertaining tribute to
a remarkable man"**

WHO
DO YOU THINK YOU ARE?.
MAGAZINE